INDEPENDENCE DAY

R E S U R G E N C E

MOVIE NOVELIZATION
YOUNG READERS EDITION

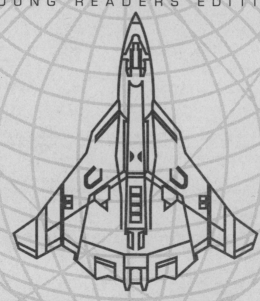

Adapted by Tracey West
Based on the screenplay written by
Dean Devlin and Roland Emmerich

Simon Spotlight
New York   London   Toronto   Sydney   New Delhi

This book is a work of fiction. Any references to historical events, real people, or real places are used fictiously. Other names, characters, places, and events are products of the author's imagination, and any resemblance to actual events or places or persons, living or dead, is entirely coincidental.

SIMON SPOTLIGHT
An imprint of Simon & Schuster Children's Publishing Division
1230 Avenue of the Americas, New York, New York 10020
First Simon Spotlight paperback edition June 2016
INDEPENDENCE DAY: RESURGENCE TM & © 2016 Twentieth Century Fox Film Corporation.
All Rights Reserved.
All rights reserved, including the right of reproduction in whole or in part in any form.
SIMON SPOTLIGHT and colophon are registered trademarks of Simon & Schuster, Inc.
For information about special discounts for bulk purchases, please contact Simon & Schuster Special Sales at 1-866-506-1949 or business@simonandschuster.com.
Designed by Nick Sciacca
The text of this book was set in Chaparral Pro.
Manufactured in the United States of America 0516 OFF
10 9 8 7 6 5 4 3 2 1
ISBN 978-1-4814-7858-8
ISBN 978-1-4814-7859-5 (eBook)

The ships had appeared out of nowhere: enormous round discs that settled above Earth's major cities and then hovered there. Most people had fled the cities, fearful of an invasion. Others had stayed to greet what they hoped were peaceful messengers from across the galaxy.

Sadly, those who stayed were wrong. The ships opened up—giant metal pieces springing open like petals on a flower—to unleash massive energy blasts on the helpless cities.

The invasion had begun. But the humans had fought back. On July 4, in a plan masterminded by scientist David Levinson, the Americans destroyed the alien mother ship and told armies around the world how to destroy the other ships. American President Thomas Whitmore fearlessly declared, "The Fourth of July will no longer be known as an American holiday, but as the day when the world declared with one voice: 'We will not go quietly into the night.' We will not vanish without a fight. We're going to live on. We're going to survive. Today we celebrate our Independence Day."

The humans won the War of 1996, but what we didn't know was that from far away, the aliens watched their defeat. And then they prepared their next move. . . .

CHAPTER 1

Twenty years later people on Earth were getting ready to celebrate the anniversary of the planet's Independence Day. At the White House—rebuilt to its former glory after the invasion had destroyed it—crews were busy preparing for the big celebration in two days.

Inside the White House, President Lanford practiced her Fourth of July speech with her team in the conference room.

"The countless lives we lost in the War of '96 didn't perish in vain. They inspired us to rise from the ashes as *one* people of *one* world. For twenty years we haven't seen any armed conflict between nations, because we put our petty differences aside. United, we rebuilt our families, our cities, and our lives. The fusion of alien and human technology not only enables us to defy gravity, it has also paved the way to create the Earth Space Defense, or ESD program, which finally makes our planet safe again."

Finished, she looked to her speechwriter and smiled. "Great speech, Patty."

"Thank you, Madame President," answered Patricia Whitmore. Former President Whitmore's daughter was only seven when the alien invasion began. She had been with her father at the time, and she knew that had probably saved her life. Her mother hadn't been so lucky. Injured in the alien attack, she had died on July 4, 1996.

Patricia would never forget that day twenty years ago. She had grown up as Washington, DC, was rebuilt. It was the only home she had ever known, and she'd moved back there after her training at the ESD Academy, choosing the White House over being a pilot in space.

Secretary of Defense Reese Tanner spoke up. "I have to disagree," he said. "This is an election year, and I strongly advise that you remind the people that you lost your entire family in '96."

The president stopped him. "Tanner, three billion people died. Everybody lost someone. We've been living in fear for the last twenty years. That ends today."

At that moment Captain Dylan Hiller, dashing in an ESD dress uniform, stepped into the conference room. He and Patricia exchanged a smile. Twenty years before, his father, Steven Hiller, had fought the aliens side by side with former President Whitmore. Dylan and Patricia had bonded during that time, and they'd remained friends throughout their childhood and then through their time at the ESD Academy.

"Captain Hiller, welcome to the White House," President Lanford said with a wide smile.

"It's great to be back," Dylan said.

"I can't tell you how proud we are to have you flying our flag up there," President Lanford continued.

"It's an honor, Madame President," Dylan replied sincerely.

President Lanford introduced Dylan to Reese Tanner. "I think you know the secretary of defense."

"Sir," Dylan said respectfully.

"Nice to see you again, son," said Tanner.

"And I don't have to introduce you two," the president said when they reached Patricia.

"Moving up in the world," Dylan said as he and Patricia hugged.

"Says America's knight in shining armor," Patricia teased.

"You're the one who's back in the White House," Dylan pointed out.

"As an employee, I don't quite get the same benefits as I did when I lived here," Patricia countered.

Dylan smiled. "How did they let us get away with everything we did?"

"Maybe it had something to do with the fact that my dad was commander in chief," Patricia replied.

An aide approached Dylan. "We're ready for you, Captain."

"Dylan, be nice to Jake when you see him up there," Patricia said before he walked away.

For the first time since he'd arrived, Dylan's face clouded. He walked beside the president and forced a smile as the camera flash popped.

Now the aide turned to Patricia. "Ms. Whitmore, it's Agent Travis. He says it's urgent."

The aide handed a phone to Patricia, and she stared at it for a moment, wearing a worried frown. Agent Travis worked for her father. When he said something was urgent, he meant it.

What was her father up to this time?

CHAPTER 2

Up on Earth's moon, workers were busy trying to get a defense cannon in place and operating in time for the big Independence Day celebration. Two crews—one American and one Chinese—had begun the operation years ago. Now it was time to see if their hard work would pay off.

Buildings on the moon base rumbled as tug spacecraft flew overhead. These were no sleek spaceships. Each one held a pilot and copilot in a boxy bubble-shaped compartment. Each tug's bulky body was designed to haul a much bigger payload across space.

In this case, the tugs were pulling a large cannon harvested from a fallen alien destroyer. The mission was simple: move the cannon onto a turret mount anchored to the moon. The mission was also tedious. The tugs had been towing the cannon for days at a snail's pace.

Inside one of the tugs, classic rock music blared. Jake Morrison, the pilot, wore a white T-shirt and a trucker cap.

"Seven miles and closing," he reported into his radio. Then he switched off the mic. "Of the slowest trip of my life."

His copilot, Charlie Miller, woke up from a nap on a bench behind Jake and yawned. While twenty-seven-year-old Jake had rugged good looks, Charlie was three years younger, as well as shorter and scrawnier.

"Remember when we thought we'd be the best fighter pilots in the world?" Jake asked. "Now we're flying fork-lifts in space."

"Hey, cheer up," Charlie told him. "There are worse things you could be doing than towing a half-trillion-dollar weapon."

"Yeah, well, I need a little more stimulation," Jake said. He got up from his chair and took a seat facing the rear of the ship, staring out at the endless space.

"You know I didn't have to follow you up here," Charlie reminded him.

"Yes, you did," Jake said with a grin. "You get lonely without me."

Charlie knew Jake was right, but he would never admit it. Both men had lost their families during the alien invasion and had been shuffled off to orphanages, where their well-meaning caretakers had tried their best to make the institution feel like home. Jake had taken little Charlie under his wing, and the two had bonded like brothers.

"I was the youngest valedictorian in the history of the academy," Charlie continued, stretching. "I could've been stationed anywhere. Like San Diego. Beaches, surfing—"

"You never surfed a day in your life," Jake reminded him.

"But I'm a fast learner, and I've got great balance," Charlie said. "Like a cat."

Jake chuckled. "Cats hate water, Charlie."

Deeper in space, more than seven hundred million miles from Earth, a crew of Russian cosmonauts was building an ESD base on Rhea, one of Saturn's moons. The view from Rhea was spectacular—Saturn's majestic rings made of rock and ice, silhouetted against the blackness of space. But right now the base was experiencing some disturbances. The Russian commander reported the power fluctuations back to ESD command.

Elsewhere on the base, the lights flicked on and off again. The heat wasn't working, and the temperature in the base was dropping by the second. Technicians hurried to locate the problem.

"The power surges blew out most of the fuses," one cosmonaut observed.

"Let's switch to the emergency generators," a tech advised.

Just then the commander came into the room. "What now?" he asked.

A third tech pointed out the window. The commander strode over. He could see a swirling, glowing mass in the sky. It seemed to be growing every second.

"Call it in," the commander ordered.

"Our communications are down," explained one of the techs.

"That's impossible," said the commander, walking over to the communications monitor.

A strange noise came over the speaker system. . . .

Back on Earth's moon, the tug pilots had the cannon in position and were getting ready to dock it into its base.

Jake carefully maneuvered his tug into position while Charlie still rambled on.

"You realize there are only thirty-six women on this moon base?" he asked.

"I'm sure one of them will eventually come around, pal," Jake told him.

"Hey, it's not like they all rejected me," Charlie protested. "I happen to have standards."

Behind Charlie, his console flickered on and off. A strange noise filled the space tug. Then the tug jolted, and the awful sound of grinding metal filled the ship.

"What did you do?" Jake cried.

"Nothing!" Charlie insisted. "Was that a power surge?"

The power was flickering on and off down on the moon base, too. A warning alarm blared.

"Sir, Tug Ten collided with the weapon!" a tech shouted.

Commander Lao looked out the window. The huge cannon was slowly falling toward the moon base.

"The clamps have stopped! They're not responding!" yelled the weapons engineer.

"All tugs, take evasive action!" Commander Lao ordered. "Pull back!"

Through his window, Jake saw the cannon falling toward the moon base.

"That's a negative, sir," Jake replied to Commander Lao.

"What do you mean, 'negative'?" asked Charlie.

Jake steered the space tug right between the moon

base and the falling weapon! Charlie shrugged at Commander Lao as they flew past the window of the moon base's command center.

"This isn't a fighter jet, Jake!" Charlie warned.

"Don't remind me!" quipped Jake.

Commander Lao's voice came through the ship's communication system. "Lieutenant Morrison, what are you two doing?"

"Improvising!" replied Jake.

Wham! Jake's space tug collided with the cannon. Sparks flew from the robotic arms, but they held firm.

The tech in the command center stared at her monitor in disbelief. "Sir! He's slowing the fall!"

Jake kept pushing the tug into the cannon. Engine warning lights flashed in the cockpit.

His crazy plan was working! The giant cannon slowly lifted back into position between the clamps.

"Commander! The locks are reengaging!" the engineer reported.

Charlie was as pale as a ghost but relieved. "Was that stimulating enough for you?" he asked Jake.

Jake chuckled. "I didn't think that was gonna work."

With one last thunk, the cannon locked into the turret.

CHAPTER 3

General Adams gazed out of the window of an ESD helicopter. The salt flats of New Mexico stretched out below him like a white sea.

The helicopter flew over a mountain, and the scene changed. Below, the remains of an enormous alien destroyer were lodged in the sand. Thousands of workers harvested pieces from the wreck, as they had been doing for the last two decades. Now mostly a skeleton of the ship remained.

Workers loaded the pieces onto trucks that carried them to the Area 51 military base. Once a top-secret alien research facility, it was now the well-known hub of all alien technology.

The chopper landed, and General Adams strode across the base, his eyes flashing with annoyance. A young man in a uniform ran to greet him.

"This better be good," Adams snapped at Lieutenant

Ritter. "My wife and I were enjoying a very nice morning at a very expensive bed-and-breakfast."

"I'm sorry, sir. I thought you should see this," Ritter said, and for the first time Adams noticed how anxious the lieutenant seemed.

He soon found out why. Ritter led him to the alien prison cells, where survivors of the crashed ship had been kept since the invasion. In the monitor center, two guards kept an eye on rows of screens showing video feeds of each alien prisoner.

"It started a couple of hours ago . . . ," Ritter began, nodding to the monitors.

Each screen showed the same thing. The aliens were shrieking wildly and throwing themselves against their cell walls, over and over and over.

General Adams frowned and gazed out of the bay window overlooking the enormous prison block.

"After twenty years of being catatonic," he muttered. "Get me Director Levinson."

"We tried. He's unreachable," the lieutenant reported.

David Levinson, Director of the ESD, was riding in a convoy of ESD jeeps heading across the African savannah as the sun set in the sky. Two United Nations armored vehicles carrying soldiers accompanied them.

Next to David Levinson, a younger guy was desperately trying to get his point across.

"The administration has made it clear that expenditures need to be reined in," the guy was saying. "And yet you've spent nearly three times your allocated travel budget this year alone."

"Who are you again?" David asked him.

"Floyd Rosenberg the accountant, sir," offered up David's assistant, who sat across from him.

Floyd kept pressing David. "I know a lot of people have a negative reaction to being audited, but it can be a very constructive experience."

"Listen, Lloyd—" David began.

"Floyd," the accountant corrected him.

David ignored him. "I have a friend I have to meet. Great guy. Come say hi."

The jeep came to a stop and David got out. The UN vehicle in front of them drove to the side, revealing the border crossing.

The sign over the crossing read, REPUBLIQUE NATIONALE D'UMBUTU. Flanking the sign were totems built from alien skulls and bones stacked on top of one another.

David smiled at two of the border guards, soldiers

wearing beige uniforms and fierce scowls. Each one of them carried a weapon—an alien blaster.

"Who are those men?" Floyd asked nervously, hurrying to catch up to David.

"Umbutu's rebel forces," David replied.

"The warlord?" Floyd's voice was shaking.

"Nothing to worry about. The old man died," David told him. "I hear his son is much more of a moderate."

He grinned at the guards again. "Howdy. I'm looking for Dikembe Umbutu."

"The one and only David Levinson!"

David recognized that French accent. He turned to see a dark-haired woman casually making her way through the crowd of soldiers.

"Catherine, wow, that's uh . . . What are you doing here?" he asked, clearly uncomfortable.

"You don't think you're the only expert he called, do you?" she asked, and he could see amusement dancing in her brown eyes.

"I'm just a little surprised to see you," he replied.

"I'm a little surprised you remember my name," she countered, and then she turned and walked off.

"So, why does Umbutu Jr. need a psychiatrist?" David asked Catherine, following her up a hill.

"His people fought a ground war with the aliens for

ten years," she replied. "Their connection is the strongest I've ever seen. It's like they're tapped into the alien subconscious."

David nodded. "Oh yeah, your obsession with the 'human-alien psychic residual condition.'"

"You're calling *me* obsessive? That's cute," she said.

They reached the top of the hill, and David's jaw dropped. Below them was a downed alien destroyer, covering the savannah for miles. This one hadn't been stripped of its parts, like most others around the world. But that wasn't what was unusual about it.

"We found something out here. Something only you might understand. The ship's been dark for twenty years," Catherine explained.

But not anymore. The destroyer's center—mile-wide pieces of metal arranged in a circle like flower petals—had opened up. Glowing lights emanated from inside the destroyer's hull.

"How did they get the lights on?" David asked.

"We didn't."

David turned to see Dikembe Umbutu standing behind him. The muscular warlord had massive machetes strapped to his back. He looked tough, but David could see worry on his face.

"It happened on its own two days ago," Dikembe said.

CHAPTER 4

Across the world, General Adams entered the Area 51 command center. The strange alien behavior had him worried, but you couldn't tell by looking at him.

Lieutenant Ritter updated him on the situation. "Our defense base on Saturn's moon Rhea has gone dark again. We haven't had contact in eleven hours."

Adams frowned. "Try bouncing the signal off one of the orbiting satellites."

"We tried that," replied Ritter.

"Then reconfigure Hubble," General Adams commanded, referring to the giant space telescope. "I want eyes on Rhea."

Back on the moon base, Jake landed the battered tug inside the shuttle bay. He and Charlie climbed out to inspect the damage. One of the tug's arms was badly bent, and the antigravity engines were smoking.

"Lao's coming in hot, and he's got that look," Charlie whispered loudly.

Jake turned to face the music. Commander Lao was marching toward them, screaming at them in Chinese.

"He knows we don't understand Chinese, right?" Jake asked.

The other tug pilots gathered around to watch the spectacle.

"That was a close call, sir," Jake told the commander.

"You almost got us all killed!" Lao screamed—in English this time.

"Yeah, but then I saved everyone," Jake countered.

Commander Lao thrust his face into Jake's. "You don't get credit for cleaning up your own mess. And you destroyed one of my tugs!" he yelled.

Jake gave a cool shrug. "That? That's just cosmetic."

Clang! Part of the engine mount fell off right as he spoke.

"Charlie can fix that," Jake said quickly.

Charlie felt guilty. He had been at the controls when the space tug banged into the cannon. He decided to come clean.

"Actually, sir, I'm the—"

"I lost my focus," Jake said quickly, before Charlie could finish. "It won't happen again."

"No, it won't," Commander Lao said. "You're grounded until further notice."

He walked off in a huff.

"You didn't have to take the fall," Charlie said.

"He already hates me," Jake pointed out. "Why break tradition?"

CHAPTER 5

Former United States President Thomas Whitmore had been out of office for roughly fifteen years. Life after the invasion hadn't been easy for him. Some said it was because one of the alien invaders had seen into his mind nearly twenty years ago. The result had left him with endless nightmares. He drew what he saw in those terrifying dreams: a circle with a line through it. Earlier that morning he had woken up, screaming from one of his nightmares. Now he roamed the streets of his Virginia neighborhood, fueled by overwhelming panic and fear.

"You weren't there!" he told two teenagers at a bus stop. "You don't understand what they're capable of!"

The two teens stepped back from the man with the bushy white beard, wearing a bathrobe over his pajamas.

"They're coming back, and this time we won't be able

to stop them!" Whitmore wailed, his eyes wild.

"I don't want to hit you because you're old and stuff, but you're big-time in my space right now," one of the teenagers said.

"Yeah, and what's up with the robe?" asked the other.

A secret service car screeched to a stop in front of them, and Patricia ran out, followed by Agent Travis. The teens stared, dumbfounded.

"All agents stand down. President Whitmore is secure," Travis said into his radio.

Patricia pulled an arm around her father and gently led him into the car.

"Come on, Dad," she said. "Let's get you home."

As they drove back to the house, Patricia tried to reason with her father. "You can't keep doing this, Dad. You need to take your pills."

Whitmore looked at his daughter with love. He knew how hard all this was on her. "I know I'm not at my best anymore. I'm sorry. You shouldn't have to bother with all this."

"It's no bother, Dad," said Patricia.

But Whitmore knew the truth. "I know you gave up flying to take care of me, Patty. I know how much you loved it."

"Yes, but I love you more," Patricia assured her father. "It was my decision. I don't regret it."

"Patty, my good days are behind me," Whitmore went on. "I did the things I needed to do in my life. You haven't yet. This is your time now; don't waste it on me. Go live your life."

After they got home, Patricia flipped open the laptop in her bedroom and saw Jake's face pop up on the screen. It wasn't easy having a fiancé on the moon, but the tug pilots could call home using video booths on the moon base.

"My dad's nightmares are getting worse," she told him.

"You still taking him to the anniversary?" Jake asked.

Patricia shook her head. "No. I want people to remember him for the man he was, not who he's become."

"You know what? I'm gonna steal a tug and come back and see you right now," Jake said.

She grinned. "Last time you did that, they added a month to your tour. I would like my fiancé back permanently, please."

Suddenly the video image on both screens wobbled. Jake could hear the white noise he'd heard aboard the space tug.

"What was that?" Patricia asked as the screen settled.

"We've been getting these weird power surges lately," Jake reported. "You take a look at the houses I sent you?"

"I haven't had a chance to, with work and everything going on," she said. "I saw Dylan at the White House today. You two have to have a conversation."

Jake was scowling. "So he gets to shake hands with the president and I'm stuck on the moon."

Patricia shook her head. "Why do you have to always be so headstrong?"

"Everyone knows he wouldn't be leading that squadron if it weren't for his father," Jake reminded her.

"You nearly killed him, remember? Give him a little credit, Jake," she said.

At that moment the screen cut out again. Jake looked into the monitor. "P?"

But all the video booths went dark, and the power flickered on and off around the base.

On Earth, Patricia slammed her laptop lid in frustration. She stared at a photo on her desk, of her, Jake, and Dylan at the ESD Academy. They all wore flight overalls and grinned in front of a human-alien hybrid jet. They had been such close friends then, and then things—well, they'd gotten pretty complicated. During their final training flight through a narrow canyon, Dylan and Jake vied for first place. Dylan was in the lead when Jake tried to pass him . . . but there wasn't enough room. Jake clipped the wing of Dylan's fighter, causing it to spin out of control. Dylan had parachuted out of the plane safely, but Jake and Dylan's friendship had died that day.

CHAPTER 6

Back in Washington, DC, Dylan's mom, Jasmine Hiller, made her rounds in the children's ward of the hospital where she worked. It was nighttime, so she moved quietly from room to room.

She checked on one young patient who was curled up, asleep, cradling a doll tightly in his arms: a Steven Hiller action figure.

The boy had left his TV on, and she picked up her remote to turn it off, when she paused. The channel on the TV was showing a retrospective of the alien invasion and the aftermath.

There on the screen, walking across the tarmac in the shimmering heat, was Steve. Jasmine froze. She knew she should turn off the TV, but she couldn't.

"Fact was, we couldn't replicate alien technology, because they grow it. But we could harvest their antigravity engines.

The 2007 test flight of the first-ever human-alien hybrid fighter was piloted by none other than the globally beloved War of 1996 hero Colonel Steven Hiller," the narrator was saying.

On-screen, Hiller got into the jet and started to climb up into the blue desert sky.

"There were rumors ESD advisers pressured for the test flight too early and fast-tracked safety inspections in order to maintain their deadline. Unwilling to risk the safety of his pilots, Hiller decided to fly the fighter himself—a decision that would ultimately cost him his life," said the narrator. *"These haunting images are forever etched into our hearts and minds, but they exposed flaws in the design that ultimately saved the lives of thousands of young pilots."*

Jasmine watched as the fighter dissolved into a huge fireball, leaving a trail of smoke. Then she closed her eyes and felt the hot tears behind her eyelids.

Jasmine and Steve had survived the alien invasion. They'd gotten married at Area 51, right before he left on his dangerous mission to blow up the mother ship. And he had survived. It was a miracle, which in Jasmine's mind guaranteed that they would live happily ever after.

And they had, for eleven years. Together the two of them had raised Dylan. Steve had risen in the ranks of the ESD. He'd been so confident before that test flight. Then . . .

Dylan was in DC right now, getting ready for a flight with the Legacy Squadron—a small team of pilots from around the world, one flyer from each country who had fought against the aliens. Jasmine's son was a great pilot, and he had just as much confidence as Steve.

That was what worried her.

Across the country, in Area 51, the sun was just starting to set. A crowd of reporters interviewed the members of the Legacy Squadron in a giant airplane hangar. Their mission later that day would be history in the making as the best pilots from countries around the world flew side by side up to the moon base.

A reporter looked at Dylan. "Captain Hiller, how do you feel taking off out of a hangar named after your father?"

"He would have loved it. It's too bad he is not here to see it," Dylan answered.

Then his cell phone rang, and he removed it from his pocket.

"Hey," Jasmine said on the other end, her voice heavy with sadness. "I just wanted to hear your voice."

"You watched it again, didn't you?" Dylan asked, shaking his head. "Mom, why do you put yourself through this?"

She ignored the question. "Just tell me you'll be careful up there."

After he said good-bye to his mother, Captain Dylan Hiller got into his cockpit and gave the signal to the other pilots. The Legacy Squadron lifted off into the sky, heading toward their destination—the moon.

Thanks to the alien technology, zipping to the moon in the hybrid vehicles didn't take long. The squadron screamed through space and headed toward the moon base.

"Moon Base, this is Legacy Squadron," radioed Dylan. "We're on final approach. Requesting permission to land."

Commander Lao's voice answered him. "Permission granted. Welcome to the moon, Captain."

The giant doors to the shuttle bay opened, and the squadron flew inside and landed. The ground crew swarmed in for autographs as the pilots disembarked.

Charlie walked in to check out the scene, and the first person he noticed was one of the most skilled pilots in the squad, Rain Lao, the pilot from China. And he wasn't the only one noticing.

Dylan walked past Rain, grinning. "When you're done being a superstar, meet us for the debriefing," he said.

As Dylan walked off, a gruff voice rose over the chatter. "Do I get an autograph?"

"Uncle Jiang!" Rain cried, throwing her arms around Commander Lao.

He stepped back. "You look more and more like your mother," he said.

Rain smiled. "There's nothing a girl wants to hear more than that."

While everyone was greeting the pilots, Jake was in the mess hall, grabbing a carton of Moon Milk from the vending machine and sitting down to eat his lunch. Charlie raced up to him.

"I've been looking all over for you," he said. "I've got good news. The pilot China sent is my future wife. I think my heart exploded. It's like our souls were communing."

Charlie noticed Dylan walk into the Mess Hall and stopped talking.

Jake didn't see Dylan, but he knew the expression on Charlie's face.

"He just walked in, didn't he?" Jake asked.

"Yes, he did," Charlie said.

Jake got up to leave and found himself face-to-face with Dylan. He and Dylan had never resolved things since—since everything had gotten messed up between them. This wasn't the time or the place.

"Mind moving?" Jake asked. "We both know what happens when you get in my way."

It was a smart-aleck comment, and Jake knew it. But he was still surprised by what happened next.

Pow! Dylan punched him square in the face, and Jake went down hard.

"Been waiting a long time to do that," Dylan said coolly.

Charlie ran to Jake and helped him to his feet just as Commander Lao marched in.

"Morrison, what's going on here?" Lao asked Jake.

Everyone waited to hear what Jake would say.

"I asked you a question!" Lao barked.

"These floors are really slippery," Jake lied. "Be careful, sir." He turned to Dylan. "Great seeing you."

Jake wiped the blood from his lip and left the mess hall. Charlie followed him to the quarters they shared.

"I was so close to punching him back," Charlie told Jake.

"I think you made the right choice," Jake said.

"It was a training accident," Charlie said. "I mean, yes, you did almost *kill* him, but that's why they have ejection seats."

"I went too far," Jake replied. "It's the only way I thought I could stand out."

"It was never gonna be you," Charlie told him. "The world doesn't work like that. He's royalty. We're just orphans."

Jake let those words sink in. "I can't believe it's been twenty years. The last thing I said to my parents was that I hated them. Only reason I'm still alive is because they dropped me off at that stupid camp."

"I'm glad they did," Charlie said, his voice starting to choke up. "'Cause you're the only family I got."

Jake almost smiled.

"And don't beat yourself up, man," Charlie told him. "Enough people are doing that already."

This time, Jake did smile.

CHAPTER 7

On the African savannah, David and Catherine rode in a pickup truck with Dikembe Umbutu. The truck came to a stop underneath one of the massive metal petals of the fallen destroyer, and the three of them climbed out.

"I appreciate you finally granting us access, Mr. Umbutu," David said. "Your father was a tenacious man who really stuck to his guns, no pun intended."

Dikembe's face clouded. "My father's pride caused the death of more than half my people, including my brother."

Catherine gazed around at the alien skulls and bones scattered all over the ground.

"Be careful," Dikembe warned.

He and David had stopped inches from an enormous hole in the ground, at least a half mile wide.

"What happened here?" Catherine asked.

"They were drilling," Dikembe replied.

"For what?" Catherine asked.

David answered. "Minerals or metals, but I don't know."

Catherine smirked. "That's a first."

"When did the drilling stop?" David asked Dikembe.

"When you blew up the mother ship," he replied.

David looked at the open core of the ship overhead. "Is there any way to get up there?"

David, Dikembe, and Catherine climbed up the fallen alien destroyer. Soon they were hundreds of feet above the ground. Dikembe and Catherine nimbly jumped over gaps and climbed up pieces of sleek metal, but David trailed behind. He'd always been afraid of heights.

They reached the ship's massive command center and climbed in. The alien technology glowed and hummed with power. David walked up to an alien console.

"It's the same pattern," he realized. "The distress call came from this ship."

David hit a few keys on the console. A holographic image of Earth's solar system appeared, floating in front of them. As Earth passed by them, they noticed a pulsating red core at its center.

"It looks like someone picked up the phone and answered," Catherine said, her eyes fixed on the core.

☆ ☆ ☆

The ship wasn't the only thing turning on again. Halfway across the world, in a hospital room on Area 51, Dr. Brackish Okun woke up in bed, screaming.

Dr. Okun had been one of the first to study the aliens, back when they were a secret. When the alien ships had come to Earth in 1996, he had been grabbed by a captured alien and linked to its mind. The experience had nearly killed him, and left him in a coma for the last twenty years, where he remained under the loving care of his boyfriend, Dr. Isaacs.

"You're awake?" Dr. Isaacs asked when the screaming had stopped.

"Where are my glasses?" said Dr. Okun.

Isaacs handed him the glasses.

"How long have I been out?" Dr. Okun asked.

"A long time, baby," Dr. Isaacs replied with tears in his eyes. "A long time."

"Yeah, I can see that," Dr. Okun said. "Babe, you got a bit fat. And really bald."

He reached up to touch his own long gray locks, and smiled with relief.

In Africa, David, Catherine, and Dikembe left the ship more puzzled than when they had arrived. They climbed back down the destroyer and returned to Dikembe's compound as the sun rose.

Dikembe lived in a sprawling house surrounded by guards and lookout towers. As they made their way to the house, Catherine showed David images on her tablet.

"This symbol comes up more than any other I've encountered," she said. "Look at the similarities. How can you not see the relevance?"

On-screen were images of symbols she'd collected from sites all over the world, and they all looked similar: a circle with a line through it. If she had seen the sketches Whitmore had been making, she would have added them to her collection.

"It's not that I don't see it," David said. "I just feel like there are more pressing matters than analyzing, uh, doodles. You know, like a giant spaceship turning back on."

David's assistant ran out of the house to meet them.

"Sir, we've lost contact with the Rhea base," he said.

"When? Why didn't you call me?" David asked.

"You left your SAT phone in the jeep," the assistant replied.

David frowned. "We have to notify the president."

"Already tried," David's assistant said. "Tanner said he'll get back to us after the press tour."

David wouldn't accept that. "During a press tour they can't take our calls? Bypass Tanner however you can."

They stepped into Dikembe's house. David's team had set up work stations equipped with monitors, satellite transponders, and other equipment. At the end of the room was a throne, and above that hung a photo of the former dictator and his two twin sons, Dikembe and his brother.

Catherine wandered over to David and showed him another image—the circle symbol painted on the side of a barn.

"The Roswell crash in '47," she informed him. "The farmer who made contact drew the same circle. And every time I interview one of my patients who had physical or mental contact with the aliens and show them this, they express one feeling. One emotion—"

"Fear," Dikembe finished for her.

They turned to him.

"And I don't think it's a circle," he continued. "The night the ship turned on, I experienced the strongest vision I've ever had."

He opened a set of massive oak doors, revealing his office. Scattered over the desk, chairs, and shelves were sketches of the same circle.

Then he pointed to a drawing propped up on an easel

in the middle of the room. It was a three-dimensional
drawing showing a sphere—not a flat circle.

"I drew this after the vision," he explained.

Catherine immediately started taking photos with her phone. David scanned the room and noticed a chart showing alien symbols with translations underneath.

"That's incredible," David said, moving closer to study them. "How'd you decipher so much of their language?"

"They were hunting us," Dikembe explained. "We had to learn how to hunt them."

CHAPTER 8

Back on Earth, at Area 51, President Lanford was walking in an airplane hangar with Secretary of Defense Tanner and speaking with reporters about her defense plan.

"On the left you'll see that our global effort to install an impenetrable network of space defense weapons has finally become a reality. In addition, the ESD is well ahead of schedule for completion of our two other defense bases on Mars, and Saturn's moon Rhea."

As she spoke, General Adams pulled Tanner aside.

"We need to cut this press tour short," he said.

"I'm sure it can wait," Tanner replied.

"It can't," Adams insisted.

Up at the moon base, Jake was trying to repair his banged-up space tug while Charlie looked on.

"You have to remove the subsonic inlets if you want to reconfigure the thermalized plasma cartridges," he lectured him.

Then Charlie spotted Rain Lao standing on the other side of the hangar.

"There she is," Charlie said in a whisper. "I'm gonna introduce myself."

He scurried off, leaving Jake alone. Massive sparks shot out of the engine. Jake scowled.

Across the hangar, Charlie walked up to Rain, who was supervising some techs rolling out a huge Chinese flag next to her fighter.

"You must be the pilot China sent," Charlie said.

"Did the giant flag give it away?" Rain asked.

"There's that," Charlie replied. "And the fact that I heard you speaking Chinese earlier. Anyway, I was wondering if you wanted to fall in love?"

Before Rain could reply to that, the lights flickered and then went out completely.

"Can someone please pay the electric bill?" Jake called out.

Outside, moon dust began to swirl and rise. Something was happening.

Inside, alarms blared and pilots and techs ran through the base.

Jake and Charlie joined the large crowd gathered in the command center. Everyone stared in awe at the sight through the bay window: a huge, swirling cloud sucking in moon dust.

"What is that?" Jake asked.

Then something began to take shape inside the wormhole.

"The object is more than thirty miles wide," the weapons technician calculated and then sent the image to Area 51 and David Levinson.

"Get me the security counsel," Commander Lao told the communications officer.

In Africa, the image appeared on a computer monitor.

"Sir, this just came in," David's assistant said.

David, Dikembe, and Catherine watched the live feed on the monitor screen. A spherical spaceship emerged from the wormhole! It began to flash in different colors, cycling through a pattern and then repeating it.

Dikembe recognized the vision that had been plaguing him.

"The vision was a spaceship," he realized.

General Adams, President Lanford, and Tanner appeared on the monitor.

"David, are you seeing this?" President Lanford asked.

"Yes, Madame President. I'm looking at it right now," David replied. "It looks like they're trying to communicate."

"They could be initiating an attack!" Tanner cried.

"Hold on a second," David said. "The design, the tech—it looks completely different than the ones who attacked us."

"At this point, we know the Rhea Base has been destroyed," General Adams pointed out. "Madame President, this could be a coordinated attack."

On the moon base, the cannon was already in firing position. The security counsel, who included leaders from China, Britain, and Russia, and Commander Lao were on the same feed as the president and David.

"Madam President, I need an answer," pressed Commander Lao.

"We should be cautious and listen to Director Levinson," said the Chinese president.

"How does the rest of the council feel?" asked President Lanford.

"Let's hold off until we know more," said the British prime minister.

"We need to be decisive. I vote to attack!" said Russia's president.

The president of France nodded. "I also vote to strike."

President Lanford was silent. She knew she was the deciding vote.

President Lanford stared at David. "David, I need you to tell me with absolute certainty that this isn't them."

David looked over to Catherine and Dikembe. Their faces told him the answer.

"I can't do that, Madame President," he said, his voice heavy.

President Lanford swallowed hard. "Take them out, Commander."

Catherine pleaded one last time. "This is a mistake! Please! They're trying to communicate with us!"

But it was too late. On the moon base, the giant cannon began to spin. An enormous jet of green light slowly built around the cannon's nozzle.

Commander Lao turned to his weapons tech.

"Fire!"

CHAPTER 9

Whoooooosh!

The green energy blast surged toward the spaceship.

Bam! The blast hit the craft head on. The spaceship spun out of control on a collision course with the dark side of the moon. It crashed into a crater, scattering in a halo of destruction.

A loud cheer erupted inside the Area 51 command center.

"It crashed into the Van de Graaff crater," Commander Lao told everyone. "We're not picking up any signs of life."

President Lanford let the reality sink in. She hoped they had done the right thing.

"You just guaranteed reelection," said Tanner smugly.

David had other matters on his mind. "Madame President, we need to send a team up to investigate the wreckage. We need to know who we just shot down."

Tanner jumped in. "The threat has been neutralized. We can send a team up, but David needs to be in DC."

"Can we not make this political?" David asked. "I need to go up there and get answers."

President Lanford gave David her answer. "You can lead a team up there after the celebration."

President Lanford walked away, and Tanner grinned at David.

"You heard her. I expect to see you next to us tomorrow, wearing your best smile," he said.

"You want to see my best smile?" David asked, and then he promptly hung up.

"Did he just hang up on me?" Tanner asked General Adams.

"Sure sounded that way to me, sir," replied the general.

On the moon base, Jake watched the exchange between David, the president, and Tanner. He had always liked Director Levinson, whom he had met through Patricia. That guy was smart.

A look of resolve crossed Jake's face. He hurried out of the moon base, followed by a puzzled Charlie.

"Where you going?" Charlie asked Jake.

"You heard it yourself. Levinson needs a ride," said Jake.

"Wait, Jake, no. We can't steal a shuttle again. Stealing a shuttle is bad." Charlie tried to reason with Jake, but Jake had made up his mind.

In Galveston, Texas, Julius Levinson stood behind a lectern in front of a crowd of adoring fans. Well, it wasn't exactly a crowd. Maybe three dozen people, give or take. And they weren't exactly adoring fans, but more like a captive audience. That was one of the upsides of booking a gig at a retirement home.

But to Julius, any audience was better than no audience. David Levinson's father had spent the last twenty years telling anyone who would listen how his son had saved the world—with his help.

Gray-haired and wearing a corduroy jacket with patches on the sleeves, Julius looked very much like an author. It also helped that he was standing in front of a large blowup of the cover of his book, *How I Saved the World*, by Julius Levinson.

"In our darkest moment, when all hope was lost, I said, 'Never give up! You have to have faith!'" he recounted. "And in that moment, *pow!* It came to me like a thunderbolt. That's when I came up with the idea that saved the world."

He waited for applause, but all he heard was snoring.

He looked at the elderly man in front of him, sleeping with an oxygen mask on.

"Are we sure he's not dead?" Julius asked. "Sir? Excuse me, sir?"

The old man opened his eyes. "Huh?"

"There he is. You didn't follow the light! Welcome back," Julius said. "Anyway, my book is a bargain at nine ninety-five. Makes a great gift for the grandchildren."

He finished the lecture and then carried the heavy box of unsold books to his car. "What's wrong with people?" he muttered. "No one reads books anymore. Maybe I should start selling online."

That night President Lanford gave a press conference from Area 51.

"At approximately twenty-one hundred hours the ESD repelled an alien attack targeting our planet . . . ," she began.

Whitmore, Patricia, and Agent Travis watched the press conference inside the Whitmore house. Whitmore picked up the remote and shut off the TV.

"It wasn't them," he said.

"You can't know that for sure," said his daughter.

"It wasn't them!" Whitmore repeated, louder this time.

Agent Travis held out a glass of water. "Sir, it's time for your meds."

"I don't need any meds!" Whitmore yelled, suddenly angry. Then he leaned back in his bed, deep in thought.

Patricia turned to Agent Travis. "Can you give us a second, please?"

The agent nodded and left.

"You shouldn't be wasting your time with a crazy old man," Whitmore said with a sigh. "You should be with Jake."

"He's on the moon, remember?" Patricia said.

"Then you should be with the president," Whitmore told her.

Patricia sat by his side and smiled. "I am with the president. And, Dad, you're not crazy."

Whitmore closed his eyes, struggling to figure out what was real—and what were simply nightmares.

"I've seen it in my dreams," he said, looking at his daughter.

"That's all they are," she told him. "Just dreams."

Whitmore shook his head. "No, Patty, they're coming back. And this time we won't be able to stop them."

Patricia looked at her father's face. She knew he believed what he was saying—and to her surprise, she believed him too.

CHAPTER 10
July 4, 2016

The sun was rising in Africa as Jake and Charlie landed a space tug in front of Dikembe's compound.

The ship's ramp opened, and Jake poked his head out.

"Someone call a cab?" he asked.

"Thanks for doing this, Jake," said David.

"Let's get moving, 'cause I kinda stole this thing," Jake explained.

David turned to Catherine and Dikembe. "Well, Catherine, good luck with everything, and let's try to keep in touch this time," he told her.

Dikembe stepped forward. "I'm coming with you."

"Oh no, no, no," David protested. "This is an ESD operation, strictly off-limits to all civilians."

But Dikembe wouldn't be deterred. "I let you in," he pointed out. "It would be wise of you to return the favor."

Dikembe walked past David and boarded the space tug.

"I'm coming too," Catherine said.

David started to protest. "Catherine—"

"Something is drawing Dikembe out there, and I'm going to find out what," she said.

She climbed aboard the tug as the accountant, Floyd, looking bedraggled, walked up to David.

"Do you know where I've been for the last fourteen hours?" he asked. "In a holding cell, waiting to get my visa so I could talk to you."

David smiled. "Why don't you join us, Floyd? Everyone else is. Might do you some good."

Then he turned his back on Floyd and climbed on board.

"No! I am not boarding that ship! And neither are you!" Floyd cried.

He turned around—and saw Dikembe's soldiers staring at him.

"I'm coming with you," he said quickly, and then joined the others. The ramp closed behind him.

Inside the tug, Jake nodded to the chair next to him. "Take a seat, David."

"Really?" David asked.

"What's the matter? You nervous?" Jake asked.

"No, it's just . . . not my favorite thing," David replied, but he sat down anyway and fastened his seat belt.

"Nothing to worry about," Jake assured him. "I haven't crashed in—well, a couple of days. But that was intentional."

"What?" David asked.

Meanwhile, Floyd was rather excited. "I have never been on a space tug. Is there anything I should know?" he asked Charlie.

"There's a lot you should know . . . ," began Charlie, but before he could say more, the engines came to life, kicking up dust behind them. The tug hovered for a moment and then sped off into the morning sky. The force pinned David back in his seat!

"That wasn't so bad," David said.

"I haven't kicked on the fusion drive yet," Jake told him.

Then Jake hit another button and they tore through space.

"*Aaaahhhhhhhhh!*" David screamed.

Down on Earth, in the Whitmore house, Patricia knocked on her father's door. There was no answer. She opened it slightly and peeked in, seeing her dad's sleeping form under the covers. She heard the TV going quietly in the corner.

"What a day it is," said the announcer. "The twentieth anniversary of the War of 1996 has suddenly become a victory celebration. Any moment now we expect President Elizabeth Lanford to go onstage."

"Dad, you awake?" Patricia asked. "I thought we could watch the celebration on TV together."

Still no answer. She walked to the bed and pulled back the covers. The blankets had been stuffed with pillows.

Her father was gone.

CHAPTER 11

At the Mall in Washington, DC, President Lanford addressed the crowd. Onstage behind her sat the members of her cabinet. A gigantic screen projected an image of the president so everyone in the crowd could see her.

Millions of people all over the world—Paris, Beijing, Rio, Dubai—gathered in their homes, their town squares, their city centers, to watch the president's speech.

"Twenty years ago the world escaped the clutches of extinction," President Lanford said. "And yesterday we did it again. Today we are honored to be in the presence of some of the brave men and women who defied insurmountable odds and led us to victory two decades ago."

After introducing some of those heroes—with David Levinson suspiciously missing from the event—President Lanford turned to look at the huge screen behind her.

Her face disappeared from the screen and was

replaced by the landscape of the moon. Massive flood-lights lit up the enormous cannon. Suddenly Dylan flew overhead with the Legacy Squad in their hybrid fighters. The crowds oohed and aahed.

"How's it looking up there, Captain Hiller?" President Lanford asked.

The screen switched to Dylan's cockpit feed.

"It's truly humbling to see how beautiful Earth is from here, Madame President," Dylan replied.

While the squadron soared across the cannon, Jake's space tug was reaching the dark side of the moon, where the sphere-shaped spaceship had crashed. He landed in the crater, and then he and David put on space suits.

The tug's ramp door opened, and the men walked out.

"What are we looking for?" Jake asked.

"The ship was trying to communicate. I'd like to know what they wanted to tell us," David answered.

Inside the tug, Dikembe stared out the window, his eyes fixed on the wreckage. The symbol of the ship had haunted him for years.

Floyd sidled up to him and noticed the tattoo on Dikembe's arm—an alien head with a row of notches stretching from the top of his arm to his wrist.

"Nice ink," Floyd said. "So all those notches represent alien kills, huh?"

Dikembe kept staring out the window.

Outside, Jake and David made their way to one of the largest pieces of the wreckage.

"Catherine, I think I just found another one of your doodles," he reported through the communications system in his space suit.

Embedded inside the wreckage was another sphere. A light flickered inside it.

David knew what had to be done. "Charlie, tell command to prep the lab at Area 51. We're bringing this thing back to Earth."

Back in Washington, President Lanford continued with her speech. "On this day twenty years ago President Whitmore declared, 'We will not go quietly into the night,' and we did not!"

The crowd cheered and then began to murmur. Someone was walking onto the stage. It was Whitmore!

President Lanford recognized him and motioned for a secret service agent to help him onto the stage.

"What a surprise! Ladies and gentlemen, another great war hero has arrived," President Lanford announced.

The crowd erupted in cheers. They wanted Whitmore to give a speech.

"Why don't you say a few words?" President Lanford asked.

Whitmore stepped up to the mic. "I just wanted to . . ."

Patricia and Agent Travis arrived. Panicked to see her father on the stage, Patricia ran toward him. And then . . .

Whitmore grabbed his head in pain and fell to his knees.

And he wasn't the only one. Up on the moon, Dikembe felt the same pain. So did Dr. Okun, in his hospital room on Area 51.

All three men had experienced psychic contact with the invading aliens before.

On the moon, the ground beneath Jake's and David's feet began to rumble. A giant shadow swept overhead, plunging the wreckage site into darkness.

The two men turned to see something enormous coming toward them. It looked like one of the alien destroyers, but this one just kept coming . . . and coming . . . and coming. . . .

"That is definitely bigger than the last one," David remarked.

The alien ship slammed through the debris field of the old mother ship, sending thousands of pieces of wreckage hurtling toward the lunar surface.

"Charlie, I think you better come and get us. Sooner the better, as in right now!" Jake yelled.

"Already on it!" Charlie replied.

He hit the throttle and lifted off just as huge chunks of broken spaceship began to rain down on them.

"Everyone, strap in! It's gonna get bumpy!" Charlie called out.

The tug was on its way—but the rain of debris was even closer. A huge piece of debris was flying right toward them just as the space tug landed.

"I got you!" Charlie cried.

He opened the ramp of the tug, catching Jake and David. Jake grabbed ahold, but David started to slide off. Jake grabbed his hand and pulled him onto the ramp.

"We're in! Close the ramp!" Jake yelled.

The ramp door closed, and David caught his breath.

Jake grabbed the controls of the tug. "We gotta move!"

"Not without that piece, Lieutenant!" David countered. He wasn't leaving the moon without the debris they had come for.

"I was afraid you'd say that," Jake said. "Charlie, get on the arms."

Charlie strapped himself into the rear turret. Jake gunned the tug, and they flew back toward the crater. Hunks of debris crashed around them as they hovered over the downed spacecraft.

The arms of the ship came down.

Kachunk! A piece of metal hit them. Charlie tried again. This time the arms grabbed the precious cargo.

"Got it!" Charlie cried.

Jake gunned the engines again as—*boom!* Another piece of debris hit them.

"Please stop hitting things!" wailed a very pale Floyd.

Charlie looked through the rear cockpit to see a big chunk of rock hurtling toward them. "There's a flying mountain coming right at us!" he reported.

Jake nose-dived the tug. "This is gonna be tight! Hold on!" He barreled toward the moon's surface, avoiding the rock. But the alien ship was another problem. It was coming closer and closer to the moon's surface. Soon there would be nowhere to run.

Suddenly the chunks of debris got sucked up against the giant alien ship. Then the ship's gravity pulled the space tug into it too!

"I can't get free!" Jake yelled. The tug was stuck to the bottom of the alien ship.

"This thing has its own gravity," David realized. "It's pulling us in."

"What does that mean?" Catherine asked.

"It means we're going for a ride, lady," Jake replied.

But being stuck to the bottom of the alien ship wasn't their only problem. On the moon base, Commander Lao was about to put the new cannon to use again.

"Fire!" he yelled.

Everyone on the space tug could see the cannon pointed directly at them.

Whoosh! The moon cannon fired. The green energy hurtled toward the ship . . . and then dissolved before it got near. An energy shield had absorbed the blast!

"Arm the primary and fire again!" Commander Lao yelled.

But then the alien ship transformed, producing its own cannon—a cannon three times as big as the one on the moon. It started to whirl, building up green energy. . . .

Boom!

One blast of the massive alien cannon disintegrated the base and sent chunks of the moon shooting into space.

CHAPTER 12

From his fighter, Dylan expertly dodged the barrage of moon debris. In her cockpit, Rain was frozen with grief for her uncle, tears streaming down her face. Dylan spotted a big chunk of the moon flying toward her fighter.

"Rain! Watch out!" Dylan warned.

Then he aimed at the debris and blasted it. It burst into pieces before it could hit her.

"Rain, listen to me. There's nothing you could have done," he told her. "All pilots, fall back."

Rain snapped out of it and sped toward Earth, along with Dylan and the remaining members of the squadron.

Back in Washington, DC, Agent Travis and Patricia scrambled to get Whitmore to safety. On the White House lawn, two aides briefed President Lanford and Secretary of Defense Tanner as they headed toward the ESD's alien-hybrid helicopters waiting for them.

"It's projected to enter Earth's atmosphere in twenty-two minutes," one of the aides was saying about the massive alien ship. "If it doesn't alter its current velocity, it could crack our planet in half."

"Initiate the orbital defense system. We will not let this happen. Throw everything we've got at them," President Lanford instructed.

One of the aides nodded and rushed off. President Lanford and her entourage boarded one helicopter while Whitmore, Patricia, and Agent Travis were ushered onto the second.

Overhead, in Earth's orbit, the alien ship was approaching the orbital defense stations. Each was equipped with a destroyer cannon.

"All orbital defense cannons, initiate simultaneous countdowns," came the order from General Adams at Area 51.

But before the cannons could fire . . . *kaboom!* The alien ship blasted them to pieces with powerful energy beams.

As Earth's defenses failed, the helicopters landed

on the tarmac at the ESD base in Maryland. The president and her staff would head to a military bunker at Cheyenne Mountain in Colorado while an ESD transport plane modified with alien tech waited to take passengers to Area 51.

Agent Travis got a message in his earpiece as they disembarked from the helicopter. "Jake's alive!" he cried. "He's with Director Levinson. They are in radio contact with Area 51."

Patricia's eyes filled with tears. When the moon base had been destroyed, she'd assumed the worst.

President Lanford and her entourage walked by, and Patricia approached her. "Madame President, can you take my father to Cheyenne Mountain?"

President Lanford nodded. "Yes, of course."

Whitmore shook his head. "I'm coming with you, Patty."

"Please, Dad, you'll be safer there," Patricia said.

Whitmore started walking to the plane going to Area 51, and Patricia sighed.

"Wish us luck," she told President Lanford.

CHAPTER 13

With the space tug still attached to the underside of the alien ship, Jake and the others focused on the view out the window. As they neared the clouds in Earth's upper atmosphere, the hull of the alien ship began to glow red.

When the ship descended over Asia, it slowed down. In Singapore, objects began to float up in the air, caught in the alien ship's gravity. Everything was ripped from the ground and sucked up into the fiery red sky.

With Singapore in ruins, the ship moved across the Middle East. It flew over the Burj Khalifa skyscraper in Dubai, an observation tower more than two thousand feet tall. The ship's gravity ripped the huge structure from the ground.

The passengers in the space tug could do nothing but helplessly watch the alien ship's path of destruction.

☆ ☆ ☆

Across the world, President Lanford's plane had landed at Cheyenne Mountain. The president and her entourage fought fierce winds as they headed toward metal doors embedded in the face of the rock.

"The alien ship touched down over the Atlantic," Tanner reported.

"Which part?" President Lanford asked.

"All of it, ma'am," he replied, and the president let that sink in. This ship was much, much larger than the one from twenty years ago.

"We have to expect major seismic activity," she reasoned. "Issue an evacuation order for every coastline."

Jasmine Hiller got the evacuation order and raced through the hospital halls, trying desperately to save her patients.

"We have less than twenty minutes to get every patient out of here!" she called in warning.

A nurse intercepted her. "We still have two in surgery."

"Get 'em in post-op as fast as you can!" Jasmine ordered as she ran into a room to find a young mother giving birth!

"Help! Help!" the woman said tearfully. "Please, don't let my baby die!"

Jasmine held her hand. "I got you, honey. You and your baby are gonna be just fine."

☆ ☆ ☆

Meanwhile, Jake, David, and the others were still attached to the alien ship. Through the window of the space tug, Jake and the others saw the petals of the ship begin to open. Suddenly everything that had been stuck to the underside of the ship began to fall back to Earth.

"What goes up must come down," David whispered. Then his stomach dropped as the tug began to fall.

"Don't worry—we're in a controlled dive," Jake assured them.

"We're falling!" David corrected him. "It's called falling!"

Down below, mayhem erupted as everything that had been sucked up now fell to Earth. With a thundering noise, the entire city of Dubai fell on London.

More objects fell as the alien ship moved. Jake expertly steered the tug between the falling debris. One huge chunk crashed into the iconic Ferris wheel that towered over the Thames River. The wheel broke apart and fell toward the water.

"Hold on!" Jake yelled.

Everyone screamed as the tug dove under the falling Ferris wheel. As they made their escape, the Petronas Towers of Kuala Lumpur in Malaysia smashed down into the bridge over the Thames.

The tug zoomed ahead, flying across the Atlantic and under the shadow of the alien ship.

"We're okay," Jake assured everyone. He turned to David. "Did you pee your pants?"

"Yeah," David answered.

"Me too," Jake admitted.

David turned to Catherine and saw that her eyes were filled with tears.

"Are you okay?" he asked.

"My mother lives in London," Catherine replied.

"Maybe she made it out," David said. Then his phone rang, and he answered it. "Dad! Where are you?"

Julius was in his fishing boat in the Gulf of Mexico. "On my boat, where else?"

"Listen to me," David said urgently. "You have to get to shore as fast as you can. Dad?"

But the line had gone dead.

A massive wall of water charged through the Gulf of Mexico. Julius strapped himself into his chair and, by some miracle, managed to ride the crest of the wave.

"Why did I buy this boat?" Julius asked himself as his boat soared high in the air.

CHAPTER 14

Dylan zipped over the Atlantic Ocean in his hybrid fighter, under the shadow of the massive alien ship. The members of the squad were supposed to meet at Area 51—but he had a stop to make.

In Washington, DC, Jasmine led the young mother, who was cradling her newborn baby, to the roof of the hospital. Jasmine's heart sank as she saw the last rescue helicopter fly off.

Then things got worse. One of the legs of the alien ship ripped through the city. Millions of tons of debris crashed into the hospital, shaking the building.

Dylan's fighter arrived just in time to see his mom and the young mother being knocked off their feet. There was no way he could rescue them in the flyer. He zoomed to the White House and made contact with a squad of helicopter pilots stationed on the lawn.

"I have bodies on the hospital roof that need immediate evac!" Dylan radioed them.

One of the pilots replied. "Negative, we were given orders to—"

"I don't care about your orders!" Dylan yelled. "Pick up those civilians!"

Back on the hospital roof, the building started to shift.

The sound of a jet screamed overhead. Jasmine and the new mother looked up to see Dylan's hybrid fighter, followed by an ESD helicopter. The chopper hovered above the roof. Then the door of the chopper opened, and a soldier extended his hand.

"Let's go! Let's go!" Jasmine yelled to the woman.

She lifted the woman and her baby safely into the chopper. Looking up, she noticed the decals on the hybrid fighter.

Dylan! she thought, relief washing over her.

Then the building collapsed underneath Jasmine. She fell along with it.

There was nothing Dylan could have done.

Across the country, a military transport plane landed safely in Area 51. General Adams saluted Whitmore when he disembarked the plane.

"Glad to have you back, Mr. President," Adams said. "It's been far too long."

"Thank you. Is David Levinson here?" Whitmore asked. He needed Director Levinson's help for what he was about to do.

"Not yet," Adams replied. "Morrison's tug is still ten minutes out."

"Have them meet us at the prison," Whitmore said. "We need to interrogate one and find out how to stop that ship."

Patricia and Agent Travis exchanged a worried look. The alien interrogation twenty years ago had almost destroyed Whitmore's mind.

General Adams escorted Patricia, her father, and Agent Travis down to the alien prison control room. Still in his hospital gown, Dr. Okun had also made his way down there. He and the prison techs were staring at the bank of monitors displaying images of the aliens in their cells. They were frenzied, shrieking and pounding their appendages against the walls.

"Why are they screaming?" Patricia asked.

"They're not screaming," Okun replied. "They're celebrating."

Patricia stared at the alien prisoners in horror. Her father wanted to interrogate them, but she knew any telepathic contact with the aliens could be dangerous. She had seen what it had done to her father before.

"How do you interrogate an alien?" Agent Travis asked.

"We can use an isolation chamber, which contains their telepathy," replied General Adams.

But there would still be risks, and Whitmore knew that . . . which was why he didn't want anyone else to go into the isolation chamber. Without their noticing, he left the control room.

In the last twenty years, great lengths had been taken to make sure the alien prisoners were secure. Each prisoner was kept in a box-shaped cell, and the cells were stacked in rows and columns in the enormous underground prison.

Whitmore approached a digital console outside the isolation chamber. He selected a cell and then stepped inside the chamber, locking it behind him.

A huge robotic arm swung across the endless rows of prison cells. It grabbed the cell and then swung back around, docking the cell to the back of the isolation chamber.

An alarm rang through the prison command center. General Adams, Patricia, Agent Travis, Lieutenant Ritter, and Dr. Okun rushed to the isolation chamber to find that Whitmore had sealed himself inside.

"Dad! It's too dangerous!" Patricia pleaded. She turned to General Adams. "We need to get him out of there!"

Lieutenant Ritter furiously typed on the console. "He overrode the system."

"Sir, please unlock the door," Agent Travis said.

"Don't worry about me," Whitmore replied. "Just get as many answers as you can."

He hit a button, triggering the sedative gas system. A thick white cloud filled the chamber, swallowing Whitmore. The others heard a hiss as the prisoner's cell door opened.

At that moment David arrived, along with Catherine, Floyd, and Dikembe.

"Whitmore locked himself in there," General Adams explained.

No one spoke as they waited to see what would happen. It was a long tense moment, and then . . .

Wham! An alien tentacle slammed Whitmore against the glass wall of the isolation chamber. Patricia felt like she couldn't breathe.

David stepped forward. "Can you hear us?" he asked.

The alien prisoner spoke through Whitmore. The president's voice sounded hoarse.

"Sheee has ariiived. Sheee has ariiived."

"Who is 'she'?" David asked.

"Sheee is aaalll."

"What does she want?" General Adams asked.

"Yoouuurrr plannnet."

Catherine held up an image of the alien symbol. "Do you know what this means?" she asked.

In response, the alien let out a piercing scream. Whitmore looked as pale as a ghost. He began to choke and shiver.

"That's enough!" Patricia cried.

"It's killing him!" Dr. Okun added.

"Get him out of there!" General Adams ordered.

Agent Travis grabbed an alien blaster from one of the prison techs.

"Move!" he yelled, and then he opened fire on the chamber.

Bam! Bam! Bam! The other guards unloaded their weapons, shattering the glass. In the blink of an eye, the alien ducked and snatched a blaster from one of the techs. It rained fire on the room.

Everyone ducked for cover—except for Dikembe. He sprang into action, unleashing his machete as he slid across the floor, under the alien's legs.

He jumped to his feet and attacked the alien, swiftly hacking off all of the creature's tentacles. Then he plunged the machete into its back. The alien shrieked, fell to its knees, and dropped the blaster.

The alien's biomechanical suit opened up, and the panicked alien inside slithered out. Dikembe finished it off with a final blow to the head.

Jake arrived as Patricia ran to her father's fallen body. "Someone, call a medical team!" she ordered.

CHAPTER 15

In Austin, Texas, a station wagon made its way through the flooded streets. A huge wave from the gulf had swept over the city, depositing wrecked boats and oil tankers into the center of town.

Four children had survived the destruction. From the car radio, they learned that the huge alien mother ship had destroyed the entire east coast of the United States. Only fifteen years old, Samantha was behind the wheel. Her thirteen-year-old brother, Bobby, sat in the passenger seat. In the back were her eleven-year-old brother, Felix, and her seven-year-old sister, Daisy, who looked like a smaller copy of fair-haired, blue-eyed Sam—except that Daisy was sobbing, and Sam was doing everything she could to keep her cool.

"Daisy, stop crying," Sam said.

"She's scared, okay?" Felix protested, patting Ginger,

the sweet, little brown dog sitting next to him.

Bobby glared at Sam. "You shouldn't be driving. You don't even have your license."

"I don't think anyone is going to pull us over," she shot back. "The radio said to head inland, so that's where we're going."

Sam steered around a wrecked fishing boat. Felix peered out his window—and saw Julius Levinson, still tied to his fishing chair!

Bobby saw him too. "There's a guy on that boat!"

"I'm not stopping," Sam said. "He's probably dead."

Bobby shook his head. "No, he was moving."

Felix leaned over the front seat. "We have to stop! He's really old. He needs our help."

With a sigh, Sam hit the brakes. Bobby and Felix ran out to the tilted boat. Felix noticed dozens of books had spilled out of it. They'd been drenched by the wave. He picked one up.

"I think he's knocked out," Bobby said, examining Julius.

Felix stashed the book in his pocket and helped his brother unlock the fishing chair. Julius hit the ground with a thud.

"If he wasn't, he is now," Sam remarked.

☆ ☆ ☆

While the Area 51 doctors helped Whitmore, David and Catherine got to work, studying the spherical spacecraft. It was still in the grip of the space tug's arms.

"I think this piece of wreckage could be the key to this whole thing. I don't think it's a coincidence it showed up right before they did," Catherine said.

Dr. Okun walked into the hangar, followed closely by Dr. Isaacs. Okun stared at the wreckage, mesmerized.

"Where did you get this?" he asked.

"From the ship we shot down," David replied.

Okun walked around it. "All the answers are in there. We have to cut it open."

A voice came over the intercom. "Director Levinson, please report to the command center immediately."

Catherine and David turned to leave. "Call us as soon as you cut it open," Catherine told Dr. Okun.

Dr. Okun waved his arms around the gathered techs. "You heard the lady! This isn't Madame Tussauds wax museum, people. Move!"

The technicians just stared at the wild gray-haired man wearing a hospital gown. Dr. Isaacs gently took him by the arm.

"Baby, I'm so happy you want to dive right back into work, but maybe we should get you some pants."

While Okun found some pants, Catherine and David watched satellite footage of the alien ship on a monitor. An infrared scan showed thousands and thousands of little dots inside the ship.

Catherine's eyes grew wide. "Are those—"

"Yes, aliens," David confirmed.

When the image reached the center of the ship, a gigantic red mass appeared.

"Enlarge," David said, and as the image got larger, they saw it was moving!

David turned to Catherine. "This must be what the alien meant by 'she is all.'"

Before he could explain, General Adams cut in.

"Director Levinson, I have the president and the remaining world leaders online," he announced.

President Lanford's face appeared on a monitor, surrounded by other leaders from around the world.

"David, what can you tell us?" President Lanford asked.

"Ma'am, we were wrong," David answered. "They're not like locusts. They're more like bees. Like a hive. And I think we just found their queen. A very big queen."

"The alien we interrogated kept referring to a 'she,'" General Adams explained. "This is the infrared image of their ship, and that's her right there in the middle."

He pulled up the image of the giant red mass in the center of the ship.

President Lanford couldn't believe what she was seeing.

General Adams typed some commands, and a shaky image appeared on one of the monitors. It showed a giant drill extending from the alien ship into the ocean.

"David, is this one of their plasma drills you briefed us about?" President Lanford asked.

"I believe so," David replied.

"Are they sucking up our water?" Secretary of Defense Tanner asked.

"No, they are drilling," David said with conviction. "We always assumed they wanted our natural resources, but I think we were wrong."

"The funnel is nearly a mile in diameter," Lieutenant Ritter announced.

"That's twenty times bigger than the one in Africa," David replied, and then it dawned on him what the aliens were doing. "I think they are after our molten core. And no core means no magnetic fields, no protection from solar radiation. Our atmosphere would evaporate. Basically, the end of life on this planet."

Shocked silence filled the room.

"How long do we have?" President Lanford asked.

"Based on the measurements we took in Africa, I'd say less than twelve hours," David replied.

The reality sank in.

"So you're saying we're already finished," Tanner said.

David shook his head. "Not necessarily. The drilling in Africa stopped when we blew up their mother ship."

The president of Russia was the next to chime in. "I don't understand."

"There must have been a queen up there we didn't know about." Then David explained what had happened back in 1996. "Assuming this hive theory holds true, if we blow up *this* queen, maybe it could work again."

"Then that's what we have to do . . . blow her up," General Adams said. "If their shield phasing is the same as last time, we can neutralize it. Then we send every fighter we've got and blanket her with cold-fusion bombs."

"How do we know this will work?" Tanner asked. "Your weapons haven't been very effective so far."

David ignored him. "Madame President, I'm afraid this is the only option we have."

President Lanford knew the future of the planet depended on their next move.

"Let's do it," she said.

General Adams nodded to Lieutenant Ritter. "Scramble our fighters!"

WE FOUND SOMETHING OUT HERE.

THAT IS DEFINITELY BIGGER THAN THE LAST ONE!

WE HAVE
TO GO!

WASHINGTON, DC

NOW IT'S A PARTY!

THEY'RE GONNA
NEED EVERY
PILOT THEY
CAN GET UP
THERE.

OUR WHOLE LIVES HAVE BUILT UP TO THIS MOMENT.

CHAPTER 16

Patricia and Jake anxiously stood watch over Whitmore, who lay unconscious in a hospital bed inside Area 51. His eyes were closed, but his fingers twitched.

Patricia turned to Jake. "I thought I'd lost you."

"Why? 'Cause the moon exploded?" Jake asked. "It'll take more than that to keep me away from you."

"I guess I should have known better," Patricia said with a grin. Happy tears streamed down her face.

Over the room's intercom, Jake and Patricia heard the order: "All pilots report to the briefing theater immediately."

"We should get suited up," Patricia said. Jake started to protest, but she cut him off. "Just because I haven't flown in a while, doesn't mean I've forgotten how."

"I know that," Jake said. He paused. "You should stay with your father."

"They're going to need every pilot they can get up there," she countered.

Jake looked into her eyes. "Please."

Patricia knew he was afraid, that he wanted to keep her safe. She looked down at her father, so helpless and fragile. She nodded, and Jake rushed off to the locker room.

Once he reached his locker, Jake looked over and saw Dylan. He had made it to the Area 51 rendezvous, but his mother had not. Jake understood his pain.

"I'm sorry," Jake said. "I know I'm probably the last guy you wanna hear from, but I've been where you are now. I know how deep it hurts. Take that pain and use it. Your mother wouldn't want you to give up now."

Just then one of the officers came into the locker room. "Dylan, General Adams is looking for you," he said. "You're leading the attack."

At first Dylan didn't say anything. He was too sad. But Jake knew Dylan had to take charge if they had any hope of defeating the aliens.

"Dylan, you have to lead us," Jake said with determination.

Dylan steeled himself. He would do what needed to be done. "See you up there," he told Jake before heading off.

A few minutes later Jake was suited up in his pilot's overalls, and he joined the others in the briefing theater.

An image of General Adams and Dylan appeared on a big screen. Beside them was a projected holograph of the alien ship, its huge red mass pulsating inside—the alien queen.

"This red mass at the center of the ship is your target," Adams said. "Analysts have confirmed that the aliens are a hive controlled by a queen who has her own protective ship. The majority of Asia, the Middle East, Europe, and parts of Africa have been destroyed. North and South America are the last continents standing. It's now up to you. Your mission is to fly cover for the bombers, who will be armed with cold-fusion warheads. The blast to her ship should penetrate the hull and kill the alien queen."

The holograph disappeared, replaced by an animation of the mission's flight path.

"Captain Hiller will brief you on the flight plan. Captain?" General Adams stepped aside.

Dylan stepped up to the microphone. As a kid, he had dreamed of becoming a pilot, like his dad. But this—this was beyond any of his dreams.

"We'll all try to converge at the same time, but whoever gets to the center first delivers the payload," Dylan explained. "We have to expect they're gonna come at us with everything they got. Protect the bombers at all cost.

"Our whole lives have built up to this moment," Dylan went on. "We've had our fingers on the trigger for a long time. I know some of you thought this day would never come. But it's here. Now we've got to step up and remind those aliens that Earth's not for the taking, 'cause I guess they didn't get the message the first time. Remember what we're fighting for. We all lost someone we love. So let's do it for them."

The pilots in Area 51 let out a cheer, and the hangar erupted into action as they scrambled to their fighters.

At the same time, Patricia left her father's hospital room and searched the hangar to say good-bye to Jake one last time. She found him and ran into his arms.

"Jake! I can't lose you again," she said.

"I'm coming back," Jake assured her. "I promise you."

Jake climbed into his cockpit. They stared at each other as his canopy closed, wondering if they would ever see each other again.

The hybrid fighters powered up and took off, one by one. Dikembe and Floyd watched from a distance.

Floyd was frustrated. He wanted to help too. He slammed his briefcase into a trash can. Then he turned to Dikembe. "Teach me everything you know."

But Dikembe just walked away.

"Yeah, well, I taught myself to solve a Rubik's Cube when I was seven," Floyd muttered. "I'll figure something out."

CHAPTER 17

Sam's fingers were clenched tightly around the steering wheel as she drove the station wagon away from the coast, out of Texas and into New Mexico. The freeway was a mess of cars full of people desperately trying to get to a safe place. Some cut through fields, others drove on the median between the lanes. Sam stayed the course, moving forward slowly and steadily.

In the backseat, Julius was squeezed in between Felix, Ginger the dog, and Daisy. He still hadn't opened his eyes. Felix searched Julius's coat pockets and found his wallet. Sam spotted Felix in the rearview mirror.

"You saved him so you can mug him?" she asked.

Felix took out Julius's driver's license and held it up to the cover of the book he had picked up by the boat. Bobby snatched the book from his brother's hand and looked at the photo. He shook Julius by the leg.

"Hey, is this really you?" he asked.

Julius woke up with a start, hitting his head on the roof. "Ouch! Where am I?"

Ginger jumped into Julius's lap and started licking his face.

"We rescued you," Daisy replied.

"What's your son like?" Bobby asked.

"Can you get us his autograph?" asked Felix. "How often do you see him?"

"Well, these days I only see him around Thanksgiving," Julius replied. "Although last year he had to cancel."

Felix was surprised. "You haven't seen him in a year and a half?"

"He's a very busy man," Julius said, and then he swiftly changed the painful subject. "What about you? Where are your parents?"

The kids got quiet. Sam finally answered him.

"Visiting our grandparents in Florida," she said, and the words hung in the air. From what they'd heard, the East Coast had been decimated by the tidal waves from the alien ship.

"I see," Julius said.

"So, where should we go, Mr. Levinson?" Felix asked.

"He's not the boss," Sam snapped. "We're going where I say we go."

Julius leaned forward, impressed by this girl who had saved her brothers and sister—and him.

"I don't want to step on anyone's toes, but the safest place to be right now is next to my David," he said softly.

Sam couldn't argue with that. She kept driving.

Area 51 wasn't far away.

At the research hangar in Area 51, Dr. Okun was hard at work, trying to cut through the wreckage that Jake and David had brought back from the moon. A crew helped him while Floyd the accountant looked on.

Okun was about to try using a diamond cutter, one of the most powerful tools known to man.

"Is there anything I can do to help?" asked Floyd.

"Yeah," said Okun. "Back off."

"Right," said Floyd. "Safety first."

Okun fired up the machine, and the blade began to lower. *Crack!* The diamond cutter was no match for the debris.

"So much for that," Okun stated.

"So what now?" asked Floyd.

Okun turned to a tech. "Do we still have the LXR-73?"

"It think it's still in storage," the tech replied.

Dr. Okun, Floyd, and the tech made their way over to

storage. The laser in question was up on a high shelf. "You couldn't leave it on the bottom shelf?" Okun complained as he climbed a ladder. "I'm coming for you, baby. There she is."

Floyd stared at the massive laser. "What is it?" he asked. "An alien laser?"

"No," Okun replied. "That's the Okun laser."

Over in the command center, David watched on a screen as the robotic drones approached the alien ship.

"Moment of truth," David said under his breath.

Several hundred drones approached the alien ship from all directions. They latched onto the green energy shield protecting the ship from attack. Then, all at once, they emitted a pulse. The shield started to evaporate!

"Yes!" David cheered, pumping his fist.

"Shields are down; you're clear to engage!" General Adams commanded.

The first wave of fighters zoomed over Washington, DC, and toward the enormous hull of the alien ship.

"Command, we have visual," Dylan reported.

The squadron reached the ship's hull and started flying up, climbing higher into Earth's stratosphere. The ship seemed to go on endlessly.

"Where are their fighters?" Charlie wondered out loud. "Why aren't they attacking us?"

"Careful what you wish for," Jake replied.

In the distance, they could see the ship starting to transform. Gigantic cannons began to emerge from the ship's hull.

Boom! Boom! Boom! The cannons shot green fire. Three of the hybrid fighters were hit, and they spiraled away through the sky.

"Evade, evade!" Dylan commanded.

Jake dove to avoid a cannon blast just as huge hangar doors opened in front of him, and hundreds of alien fighters came flying out.

Jake had never seen anything like them before. They didn't look much like the flyers from twenty years ago. These looked sleeker, and they were much faster and more agile. They aimed a barrage of fire at the hybrid fighters, and four more went down.

Dylan zigzagged through the alien fighters, returning blasts at amazing speed, taking out one after another. Out of nowhere, three alien fighters converged on his tail.

Boom! He took one out quickly, but the other two stuck to him like glue.

Suddenly he saw one of his own fighters racing right toward him. It was Jake! He fired inches above Dylan's

fighter, exploding the two alien ships into fireballs.

"You can thank me later!" Jake told him.

"I'll thank you right now!" Dylan responded.

But most of the action wasn't going their way. Jake watched as one of the hybrid bombers exploded next to him.

"Command, we can't get to the top of the ship," he reported. "It's too heavily armed. We're dropping like flies here!"

As Jake flew past the open doors to the hangar hull, an idea struck him. "I think we need to fly inside! Lieutenant Miller and I request permission to enter the enemy ship."

"We do?" Charlie asked.

Dylan looked at the open bay doors and saw that Jake was making sense. "Morrison's right. It's our only shot."

General Adams nodded. "We'll trigger the bombs from the command center so we can give you enough time to get out of there."

"Jake, follow my lead," Dylan said as he roared toward the alien ship.

At that very moment Whitmore bolted awake in his hospital bed.

"She knows!" he yelled.

Patricia and Agent Travis rushed to his side.

"Patty, you have to warn them!" Whitmore cried. "Please—she knows they're coming!"

Dylan's squad flew into the alien ship through a long series of tunnels. They emerged into the center, an enormous dome hundreds of miles wide. There the pilots could see a huge drill, pumping a glowing orange fluid through the ship's machinery.

"We got eyes on the target. Tallyho. Open bomb bay doors," commanded Dylan.

"This is too easy," Jake muttered to himself.

Back on Earth, Patricia ran into the Area 51 command center. "Get them out of there! It's a trap!" she yelled.

But she was too late. A giant pulsing light emanated from the dome inside the alien ship. Jake's engines cut out.

"Command, I have engine failure," he reported.

"Me too!" Charlie added.

All the fighter planes—hundreds of them—and the bombers began to free-fall down the center of the dome, plummeting into a ten-mile drop.

"We're falling," Jake radioed. His breathing got heavy as the g-force pressed down on him. "Everybody . . . is going . . . down. You have to . . . trigger the bombs! It's the only way!"

Patricia listened, terrified.

Dylan's fighter was in free fall like the others. He watched helplessly as pilots ejected from their cockpits all around him. "Don't l-let us . . . die for nothing," he said.

David and Patricia looked at each other, devastated.

General Adams knew the men were right. "Initiate detonation."

The bombers opened their bay doors, revealing their payload. Instantly metal alien spheres came flying toward the bombs and latched on—but none of the plummeting pilots noticed.

Back in the command center, Jake's strained voice came over the radio.

"Tell P . . . love . . . her!"

"I love you," Patricia whispered, tears streaming down her face.

Lieutenant Ritter counted down to the detonation. "Three . . . two . . . one . . ."

Woooooomp!

The bombers erupted in blinding white light—but the metal alien spheres formed bubblelike shields around each explosion, containing the blasts!

"N-negative impact!" Jake reported as his plane broke apart around him. "The bombs were contained . . . by an energy shield!"

Then he ejected from his flyer.

"Eject! Eject! All pilots, eject!" Dylan said.

Shock could be felt throughout the Area 51 command center. The alien ship had not been destroyed. Their plan had failed.

"Something's happening!" one of the flight officers cried.

The hangar doors on the alien ship closed. Then a smaller door opened, and a large alien object shot out. It exploded into a beam of energy that raced around the circumference of the Earth, decimating every satellite in orbit!

One by one, the monitors in Area 51 fizzled out, followed by the lights. As the emergency lights kicked in, David sank into a chair, defeated.

"She baited us," he said, realizing what had happened.

CHAPTER 18

Sam slowly drove the station wagon down a New Mexico highway. The car's fuel gauge was almost on empty, and she had hoped to fill up at the next rest station. But the line to get gas was a mile long.

"There're, like, a thousand cars," Sam said, frustrated. "We'll never get gas."

"Have a little faith," Julius told her.

Sam's head snapped around. "Really? You want to talk about faith? My parents are probably dead right now, and most of my friends—"

A dam broke inside Sam, and the emotions she'd been holding back rushed through. She burst into tears.

"Pull over here," Julius said. "Get a little air."

Sam obeyed. She got out of the car and stared at the horizon. Julius joined her.

"I'm really sorry for everything you're going through,"

he said. He looked back at the car. "But look, your siblings are still here. And so are you."

Sam didn't respond.

"I lost David's mother when he was very young," Julius said. "I didn't think I could go on, but I knew I had to, for him."

Sam turned to face him. "What's your point?"

"You're gonna have to do the same thing for your little brothers and sister," Julius replied.

A gas station attendant walked by. "We're all out! Pumps are dry!"

"Why don't you let me drive and you can take a little break?" suggested Julius.

Sam didn't argue. In fact, she smiled. "You would've been a good grandpa."

Julius took the driver's seat and resumed the journey to Area 51. He left the freeway and took a side road, driving as slowly as possible. Angry drivers passed by, honking their horns.

"If we go any slower, we'll be going backward," Bobby complained from his new perch in the backseat.

"We have to conserve our gas," Julius explained.

"Area 51 is still seventy-five miles away, and we're running on fumes," Sam added.

A minute later they slowly came up to a school bus

stopped on the side of the road. The words *Camp Jackrabbit* were painted on the side, and about a dozen kids were standing outside, each one of them wearing rabbit ears. Julius pulled to a stop beside them.

"Who's in charge here?" Julius asked.

"No one," replied a camper. "Our driver left us to take a ride to Minnesota."

Julius was horrified. "He left you? Just like that?"

Julius got out of the car and stepped onto the bus. He turned on the ignition, and the gas gauge showed a tank that was almost full. He stuck his head out the window. "All aboard!" he called out.

"What about our car?" Sam asked.

"We'll get you a new one when you get your license," Julius said. "Everyone, in! We're off to see the wizard!"

CHAPTER 19

Deep inside Cheyenne Mountain, President Lanford had monitored the attempted attack on the alien mother ship from the control room. But since the satellites went out, they had had no further contact with Area 51.

"Tanner, we need a status report," President Lanford ordered.

"We're trying," he replied, "but all satellites are down. We're completely blind."

Wham! The room shook as dust rained down and part of the ceiling collapsed on them.

Womp! The doors blasted open. When the smoke cleared, four aliens burst into the room—tall creatures with extra-long limbs, huge eyes in a narrow face, and a large flat skull-pan extended from the back of the head. They headed straight for President Lanford.

"Leave them alone," President Lanford said, her

voice strong and brave. "I'm the one you want."

"No! Stay behind me, Madame President!" Tanner yelled.

He started blasting at the aliens. Other secret service agents opened fire as well, but they couldn't penetrate the aliens' biomechanical suits. Tentacles shot out from one of the aliens, grabbing Tanner by the neck. . . .

Back at the research hangar at Area 51, Dr. Okun was getting his laser ready. "Careful! Don't agitate the crystals!" he told the techs. Then he turned to Floyd and explained about the laser. "Built it back in '94. Had to shelve it, though, after the meltdown in Sector G."

Floyd frowned.

Dr. Isaacs wasn't too thrilled about his boyfriend's plan either. "Baby, you're exerting yourself," he cautioned.

But Okun wouldn't hear of it. "Be a good boy. Stand over there."

"What meltdown? Are we sure this thing is safe to use?" asked Floyd.

"Highly unlikely," Okun answered as he pulled his goggles down over his eyes. "All clear!"

Floyd backed away as the laser began to cut.

Lieutenant Ritter, followed by two ESD soldiers,

walked into the Area 51 command center. General Adams turned and saw that one of them was carrying a Bible—and the other a black satchel containing the "nuclear football." Inside it was a device that the president of the United States could use to authorize the detonation of a nuclear bomb.

His heart sank. There was only one reason they would be carrying those items.

"General, Cheyenne Mountain is gone," he said. "All seventeen members of the presidential line of succession are presumed dead. To the best of our knowledge, you're the highest ranking officer still alive. The ESD is here to swear you in, sir. Attention to orders!"

General Adams placed his hand on the Bible. He swore to preserve, protect, and defend the Constitution of the United States.

He just hoped there would be a country left to defend. After all, the drill on the mother ship was still operating. The Earth's molten core—and all life on the planet—didn't have much time to spare.

Jake released his parachute as he plummeted through the center of the alien ship. Then he blacked out.

When he opened his eyes again, he found himself

dangling from his parachute, which had hooked onto some kind of giant machine. Below him was a marshy field of alien plant life. He blinked.

The sound of human screams and alien blasters jerked him awake. He unbuckled himself and fell with a splash into the marsh. When he stood up, he was up to his knees in water.

Bam! Bam! Bam! The air around him erupted in weapons blasts, and he turned to see a wave of alien soldiers behind him, firing their weapons at him.

Suddenly someone tackled him, pushing him away from the blasts. It was Dylan!

Bam! One of the laser rounds hit Dylan's leg, but that didn't slow him down. He led Jake to some overgrowth, and the two pilots hid.

"We need to get out of here," Jake said, but for the time being, there was nowhere to run. Jake and Dylan held their breaths as a group of alien soldiers marched past. Once they were far enough away, Jake and Dylan cautiously emerged. Their mission now? Find a way out of the alien ship.

CHAPTER 20

Over in the Area 51 research hangar, Dr. Okun was beginning to feel a real sense of hope—his laser was working, slicing open the wreckage.

Clang! A perfectly round silver sphere clattered to the ground and rolled toward him.

"Hello, gorgeous," Dr. Okun said. "It's time to find out what secrets you're hiding." He turned to his team. "Let's find out what we're dealing with. Get everyone down here."

Nearby, David walked through the nearly empty aircraft hangar. A few mechanics and other soldiers were left, but without the pilots, it felt eerily quiet.

"David."

David turned to see Whitmore standing there.

"Ah, President Whitmore!" David said with respect. Then his face clouded. "I had twenty years to get us ready. We never had a chance."

"We didn't last time, either," Whitmore pointed out. "We always knew they'd be coming back. We've been waging this war in our heads for too long. But look how far we've come. In the last twenty years, this planet has been unified in a way that's unprecedented in human history. That's sacred. That's worth fighting for."

A nearby soldier stopped working to listen to Whitmore. A few others also turned their attention to him.

"And that's worth dying for," Whitmore continued. "We convinced an entire generation that this was a battle we could win. And they believed us. We can't let them down."

Just then Catherine and Dikembe came rushing toward them.

"David, Dr. Okun got it open!" Catherine cried.

David, Dikembe, Catherine, and Whitmore hurried to the research hangar. When they arrived, they saw the silver sphere. Dr. Okun was feverishly working behind a large computer console. He nodded when he saw them.

"You guys have to see this," he said, and the others rushed to look at his screen.

"I've run every possible scan, and it's not giving off any kind of signal," Okun reported. "I mean nothing. It's as though this thing doesn't exist."

"Almost like it's trying to hide itself," David said.

"It's really smooth."

They turned to see Floyd standing next to the sphere. The accountant was touching it!

"You're not wearing gloves! You'll contaminate it!" Okun warned.

"Remove your hands, Floyd," David said calmly.

Floyd tried and then frowned. "That's weird. I can't."

Suddenly the sphere swallowed his hands! They disappeared inside the silver ball!

"Okay, I'm trapped now!" Floyd yelled in a panic. "Can someone please do something? It's swallowing me!"

Everyone rushed to his side.

"Just stay calm and don't panic," David said.

"This thing is trying to eat me, and your advice is not to panic?" Floyd shrieked.

Womp! It released Floyd, and then the sphere began to hover above the floor.

Meanwhile, President Lanford had blacked out when the alien soldiers had grabbed her. She awoke to find herself on the floor of a strange dark room. She slowly sat up.

Part of her brain realized she wasn't in Cheyenne Mountain anymore. That she was likely on the alien mother ship.

Another part of her brain desperately hoped that wasn't true.

"Tanner?" she called out.

She heard a movement nearby, but she couldn't see anyone in the darkness. Out of the shadows, Tanner slowly made his way toward her. Then she saw it—a giant tentacle was wrapped around his neck, holding him up inches above the ground.

All her hope shattered.

"*Wherrrrrrre is it?*" It was Tanner's voice, but it sounded strangled. President Lanford knew the alien queen was speaking through him—that was how these aliens worked.

A holographic image popped up in front of President Lanford, showing the spherical spaceship.

"We shot it down. It crashed on the moon," President Lanford answered.

"*Not the shiiiiiip. I waaaaant what waaaas insiiiiide,*" the queen said.

A massive alien head descended from the shadows and loomed over President Lanford. "I don't care what you want," President Lanford said bravely. "I know I won't live to see it, but we're going to beat you again, you ugly beast!"

An alarm began to sound. The alien queen's head

jerked up as an image appeared on a monitor. It was of the same symbol that Catherine and Dikembe had been wondering about—the symbol of the sphere the queen was looking for. The queen screeched. The human leader was no use to her now. She terminated her quickly, and from a hatch in the ceiling, a huge mechanical suit began to descend. It was armor fit for a queen.

CHAPTER 21

Not too far away on the alien mother ship, Jake, Dylan, and some other pilots were gathered at the edge of the field, at the base of one of the enormous columns. Dylan looked up to see huge landing platforms overhead.

"We need to get up there," he said.

"Then steal their fighters and get out of here," Jake added.

At that moment an alarm blared, and the alien queen's personal ship flew out of the mother ship. Other aliens climbed into their fighters and followed their queen. The hangar doors opened and they took off, heading toward Earth.

"It looks like they're mobilizing," Dylan reasoned.

☆ ☆ ☆

At Area 51, David carefully walked around the sphere, studying it. President Adams and Lieutenant Ritter walked in moments later, followed by a security team.

"This thing better not be a Trojan horse, David," the new president warned, referencing the Greek myth where soldiers tricked the enemy into letting them into their fortress by hiding in a giant wooden horse.

"I don't think it's a danger to us," Catherine said. "But it might be to them."

Dr. Okun nodded to Floyd. "He turned it on just by touching it."

Suddenly the sphere began to speak. A voice emanated from it.

I activated myself when I detected your biological signature to be different from theirs.

"It speaks! In English!" Okun exclaimed.

I deconstructed your primitive language.

"We're primitive?" Dr. Okun felt a little insulted.

Correct. My species shed our biological existence for a virtual one, thousands of years ago.

"It's a floating supercomputer!" Floyd marveled.

That is an underestimation of my capacities. I carry the combined intelligence of my entire species.

Dr. Okun nodded. "Far-out."

David raised an eyebrow. "Why are you here?"

Of all the species in all the galaxies they've faced, you *are the only ones who have ever beaten them. When I intercepted their distress call, I knew they would come to exterminate you. I came to evacuate as many of you as possible.*

"Why did they come now?" David asked. "After twenty years?"

Time is relative in space travel. Twenty years for you was only days for them. I tried to warn you, but you attacked me with the same weapons they used on us.

"They attacked you?" David asked.

Correct. A harvester ship conquered our planet and sucked out its molten core.

A holographic image projected from the sphere. An alien drill ship latched onto a planet's surface and began to suck out the planet's magma. Roots began to form and grow from its legs. As the ship sucked up magma, the roots grew and changed, forming an alien mother ship!

They use planets' cores to refuel their ships and grow their technology. They have done this to thousands of species. They are the end of everything.

More images projected from the sphere—a great battle of spheres and alien ships exchanging laser blasts against the darkness of space. Only one lone sphere escaped, zooming across the universe.

I was the sole survivor.

"Do you have a plan?" David asked.

There is a planet where survivors from other fallen worlds work to build weapons to defeat them once and for all. Your victory was our inspiration. But now that I am activated, the queen will detect my signature and hunt me down.

Because of their psychic contact with the aliens, Dikembe and Whitmore knew what the sphere was saying was true.

The wheels in David's head were beginning to spin. "What happens when we kill her?"

No one has ever killed a harvester queen.

"That's encouraging," Okun remarked.

But the sphere took a guess at what would happen if the people on Earth succeeded. *As a hive, I believe her soldiers will fall. But it's too late now; you must terminate me or she will get the coordinates to the refugee planet. And that will be the end.*

David's eyes lit up. "Wait a second," he said, pacing back and forth. "If we're so sure she's coming here, maybe we can bait her like she baited us."

A small ray of hope started to grow. They had the start of something.

David and Dr. Okun quickly got to work on the plan of attack. President Adams walked up to check on their progress, followed by Lieutenant Ritter.

"Dr. Okun thinks we can replicate the sphere's RF radiation signal . . . ," David began.

"English, please," President Adams said.

"Every computer emits a radioactive signature, whether it's your laptop, your phone, even your watch," Dr. Okun explained. "The sphere has an RFR that's completely off the charts."

"We think this signature is what their queen detected when we unlocked it," David continued. "If we put the sphere inside the isolation chamber and pack the decoy transmitter on a tug loaded with cold-fusion bombs—"

"We can fly it up her royal butt, and bon voyage!" Dr. Okun finished cheerfully.

President Adams frowned. "You set off cold-fusion bombs, and you'll kill everyone from here to Houston!"

"Not if we use the shield generators from the base to contain the blast," David said.

President Adams turned to Lieutenant Ritter. "Without our shields, we are going to need to put an alien blaster in every able-bodied hand."

"Now we just need a way to see her coming," David said.

President Adams nearly smiled. He had an idea for a solution.

David followed the president to an old storage hangar. Soldiers whipped a dusty tarp off an old radar truck from the 1950s. It didn't rely on satellite technology, so it would work for them despite the alien sabotage of all satellites.

"It was supposed to go to the Smithsonian Museum," President Adams said.

David nodded toward two soldiers. "Drive it to the highest point. The higher the better."

Area 51 started to hum with activity as everyone got ready for the plan, their hope renewed.

In the pilot's locker room, Whitmore walked between the flight banks, looking for something. Agent Travis followed closely behind him, as always.

Whitmore stopped when he found an open locker containing a flight suit. He caught an image of himself in the locker mirror and frowned. Who was this man with the crazy beard? He didn't recognize himself.

Then he spotted a shaving kit. . . .

In the aircraft hangar, techs finished attaching the reassembled pieces of wreckage onto a space tug. Dr. Okun placed a decoy transmitter inside the wreckage. Other techs loaded cold-fusion bombs onto the tug.

President Adams and David briefed a small crowd of pilots, including Patricia, who had suited up once the plan was announced.

"The idea is to bait her into following us into the salt flats, using this decoy transmitter," David explained.

"Once she's taken the bait, our cold-fusion bombs will go to town. It can work. It has to. We have less than two hours until the Earth's core fails."

"Let's get it done," Patricia said.

"There's a catch," David said. "They took out our satellites, which means someone is going to have to fly it manually."

A grim silence set in. Whoever piloted the tug would not be coming back.

"I know we're asking you for the ultimate sacrifice, but you're the only pilots we have left," President Adams said. "And I need a volunteer."

Whitmore walked up, clean-shaven and dressed in a flight suit.

"I'll do it."

"Dad, what are you doing?" Patricia asked her father. Then to President Adams, she said, "Sir, he's in no shape to fly. This mission is too important. We can't have him compromise it." Even as she said the words, she knew they weren't true. But the thought of losing her father . . .

Whitmore spoke softly. "Patty, there are a lot of reasons why I'm the best choice for this. You have to pick up the pieces when it's over. This is my part."

He turned to President Adams, who nodded respectfully. Then Whitmore walked away.

Patricia turned to Agent Travis. "Do not let him get on that tug. Do you understand me?"

"Who's going to replace him?" Travis asked.

Her expression was as solid as steel. "I will."

CHAPTER 22

Down in Area 51, President Adams hovered by an old-school radar screen set up in the command center. His soldiers had parked the truck on a nearby peak and had powered up the radar dish.

Catherine and Lieutenant Ritter flanked the new president. The radar screen came to life, and a large blip showed the alien queen's ship entering the air space, surrounded by her massive attack force.

"David, they're coming in fast," President Adams said over the radio.

David was racing across the New Mexico salt flats in the lead truck of a convoy carrying the shield generators.

"Give me numbers, Mr. President," David said.

"Nine minutes to the queen's ship's arrival. Twenty-two minutes before the Earth's core fails," Adams told him.

David radioed the other trucks. "Take your positions."

The trucks drove away in different directions, moving to place the shield generators in a wide circle around Area 51.

Not far away, Julius drove the school bus filled with campers and Sam and her siblings. They headed across the salt flats toward Area 51.

Some of the campers were reading Julius's book.

"It says you got to fly on Air Force One," said one kid.

"You met the president?" asked another kid.

"My father says your son never went to space and it's a conspiracy," piped up another.

"Is that right?" Julius asked.

Suddenly a strange high-pitched hum came from behind them. Seconds later a wave of alien fighters streamed overhead.

"Oh boy," said Julius. "Hold on to your seats!"

The enormous shadow of the queen's ship glided over them, plunging the school bus into darkness. Julius held his breath. To his relief, the queen and her army moved on, ignoring them.

Back in the alien mother ship, Jake and Dylan continued to climb up the tall column, leading the other pilots. They stopped on the last ledge underneath the flight platform. It was finally in reach, but they could hear something above.

Suddenly Charlie's head popped down from the flight platform overhead!

"Jake!" Charlie cried happily.

Jake jumped, almost falling off the ledge. "Hey! That's a heck of a time to scare a guy."

"Sorry," Charlie said.

The two friends briefly stared at each other. Jake felt like a missing piece of himself had been reattached.

"It's good to see you," Jake said. "I didn't think you'd make it."

Charlie was mildly offended. "Why not?"

"Oh, you know," Jake replied. "You haven't flown a fighter in a while, and—you're alive. That's what counts."

Then they heard Rain's voice coming from the platform.

"Enough with the reunion!" she hissed. "They are gonna hear us!"

"More of us made it!" Charlie told her.

"You're still talking loud," Rain reminded him.

Jake, Dylan, and the other pilots climbed up onto the flight platform and scurried toward Rain. She had taken cover inside a troughlike indentation. From there, they could see that only a few alien fighter planes remained. Most of the alien soldiers had taken off, but a few were left, and they could see several of them inside a control station.

"So what now?" Charlie asked.

"Whatever we do, we gotta move fast," Dylan pointed out.

To the astonishment of the others, Jake started walking toward the control station.

"What are you doing?" Dylan asked.

"You guys, get to those fighters and don't leave me hanging," Jake replied.

Then he stepped out into the open, waving his arms.

"Excuse me! Down here!" he called out.

The aliens heard him and turned, screeching. With the aliens' attention fixed on Jake, now Charlie, Rain, and Dylan could make a dash for two of the fighters.

Then two doors hissed open at the base of the control station, and a platoon of aliens streamed out, shooting at Jake! He sprinted down the flight deck and took cover inside another utility trough.

Bam! Bam! Bam!

An alien fighter plane swooped in, blasting away at Jake's attackers. He looked up to see Rain piloting the ship! Charlie was in the gunner seat, doing all the damage.

One of the alien soldiers was hit but still alive. Wounded, it crawled toward its weapon.

Jake bolted up, ran to the alien, and clocked him with a right hook. The alien recoiled and then lurched forward, completely unaffected by the punch.

The alien reached his weapon and pointed it at Jake. But before he could fire—

Bam! Dylan blasted the alien from another alien fighter plane.

Jake made a run for Dylan's plane. He jumped inside and switched seats with Dylan. Dylan would fly and Jake would shoot.

They lifted off and flew toward the opening at the end of the hangar. But it was closing quickly.

"If we don't make it out of here, I just want you to know I'm really sorry for almost killing you during training," Jake told Dylan.

"If we don't make it out of here, I just want you to know I'm not at all sorry for hitting you in the face," Dylan teased.

Jake smiled. It was good to be friends with Dylan again.

Dylan and Jake, with Rain and Charlie, fought off alien fighters as they tried to reach the opening. Lasers cut through the air at every angle. Rain and Dylan piloted their ships as fast as possible while trying to avoid being hit.

After an intense battle, the pilots were clear of the alien fighters. It was time to get out of there! Rain, with Charlie still in the gunner seat, piloted her ship out first.

"Hold on to your seat, buddy!" Dylan told Jake as he made a last-ditch effort before the doors closed and they were trapped inside the alien mother ship forever.

From outside the ship, Charlie was getting nervous. "I don't see them," he fretted.

"You miss me?" said someone outside Charlie's line of vision. It was Jake! "I told you you'd get lonely without me."

Charlie laughed with relief.

Dylan took the lead. "All right, aviators. Let's turn and burn. Clock's ticking; gotta move."

CHAPTER 23

There were only twelve minutes left until the Earth's core was breached. It was time for President Adams to address the team. He spoke into a microphone set up to radio stations at Area 51 and around the world.

"Ladies and gentlemen, make no mistake. This is humanity's last stand . . . ," he began. "What we do in the next twelve minutes will either define the human race or finish it. I understand that some people around the world are tuning into this channel on their shortwave radios. To those of you listening, no matter your nationality, color, or creed, I ask that all of you pray for us. No matter our differences, we are all one people. Whatever happens, succeed or fail, we will face it together, standing as one."

Around the word, those listening nodded. The time was now.

"They're gonna target the cannon first," President Adams radioed to the cannon crew. "We won't be able to get too many shots off, so make them count!"

Zoooooom! The alien fighters flew in, unleashing a barrage of laser fire. Several of the smaller buildings on the base exploded into flames.

The cannon crew fired up the destroyer cannon. It hummed and whirled, and then . . . *boom!* It wiped out dozens of fighters in one shot, blasting through their protective shields.

On the radar screen, President Adams could see the queen's ship coming closer and closer.

Down in the alien prison, Dr. Okun's tech finished sealing the isolation chamber. The real sphere would now be safe there. He radioed President Adams and let him know.

"Tom, we're ready at our end," President Adams relayed to Whitmore, who was in position in the pilot's seat of the tug carrying the decoy transmitter—and the cold-fusion bombs. He was surrounded by a squadron of fighters who would ensure he made it to the queen's ship safely.

President Adams gave the order. "Activate the decoy transmitter on my mark. Three . . . two . . . one . . . mark."

Roar! Whitmore gunned his engine and zoomed out of the hangar and into the action.

"The convoy is a go!" President Adams radioed the cannon crew. "Give them cover fire . . . now!"

"I'd forgotten how much fun this is!" Whitmore yelled into his transmitter.

The giant cannon blasted a path through the alien fighter jets. The convoy safely flew through the jets, moving toward the salt flats.

President Adams and Catherine watched the space tug blip move across the radar screen. Would the queen fall for the trap?

But the alien queen's ship kept getting closer and closer to Area 51.

Then suddenly the blip on the screen made a sharp turn and started following the decoy!

"It's working!" Catherine cried. "She's following the decoy!"

At the same time, Dr. Okun moved to put his hands on the alien sphere.

"What are you doing?" Dr. Isaacs asked him.

"It's isolated, so I'm going to turn it back on," Okun replied.

Isaacs looked puzzled. "Why would you do that?"

"To see what else this thing knows," Okun said, his

eyes shining. He put his hands on the sphere.

"Excuse me, gorgeous . . . ," Okun began. "But I have a few questions if you don't mind—"

Womp! The sphere began to hum and hover. A hologram burst from it, showing complex star charts and machinery like nothing any human had ever seen.

Dr. Okun looked at it in awe. "This is going to catapult our civilization by thousands of years. Our understanding of space-time, physics, fusion energy, wormholes—"

"Calm down, honey," Dr. Isaacs interrupted.

"I don't want to calm down!" Dr. Okun protested.

Outside, David worked feverishly to get the shield generator operating. One of David's techs tossed him some binoculars.

"Sir! There is a school bus headed right for the trap!"

David looked through the binoculars to see a yellow school bus headed into the middle of the energy shield.

He ran toward the bus, waving his arms. The bus kept coming.

Sam leaned over to Julius and pointed at the windshield. "There's a tall gangly man trying to wave us down."

"Tall and gangly?" Julius's eyes lit up. "That's my David!"

Julius pulled the bus up to David's mobile tech station. He got off and ran to his son.

David was shocked. "Dad?"

"David!" Julius cried with glee. "It takes the end of the world to get us together? Come and give me a kiss already!"

"Uh, Dad, not now," David said, furiously typing into his monitor.

All the kids were staring at the famous David Levinson.

"You'll be happy to know I made a few acquaintances," Julius chatted, motioning to the kids.

"I'm a little busy right now," David said. "Look!"

Julius looked up to see the huge ship of the alien queen approaching.

Overhead, Patricia pulled her fighter up to the right of the space tug.

"You didn't even say good-bye," she radioed her father.

"You wouldn't have let me go," Whitmore replied.

"You should have let me do this," she insisted. "You've done enough. You don't have to save the world *again*!"

"I'm not saving the world, Patty," Whitmore confessed. "I'm saving you."

Patricia didn't know what to say, so Whitmore continued. "It's good to see you flying again. Your place is in the air."

Suddenly Whitmore noticed that the tug's control cut out.

"I've lost manual control. The queen has locked onto me. Patty, go!" Whitmore ordered.

A giant hatch opened in the underbelly of the queen's ship. A tractor beam shot out and began pulling the tug in.

Patricia watched her father go, but then his head snapped back.

"She's in my head!" her father cried. "She knows it's a trap!"

CHAPTER 24

Alien fighters began to swarm around the tug, firing. The hatch in the queen's ship began to close. Whitmore wouldn't make it in with the bombs!

Whitmore knew what needed to be done. "Can you get me to the target?" he asked his daughter.

"Yes, sir," she replied. She caught up to the tug and blasted at the alien fighters, creating a path for her father to make it to the queen's ship before the door closed. Father and daughter made a great team.

"It's your time now, Patty," Whitmore told her as he sneaked through the closing doors. "I love you."

"I love you, Daddy!" Patricia told him as she watched him fly into the ship. She steered away, tears in her eyes.

On the ground below, David waited until he saw her plane escape the trap zone that had been set up to ensnare the queen.

"Now! Now! Activate!" he radioed.

The generators roared to life, and an enormous shield popped up around the desert like an energy dome. The queen and her fighters had almost reached the shielded area.

Inside the queen's ship, Whitmore looked through the cockpit to see two enormous legs in front of him. As the tug was slowly pulled upward, he came face-to-face with the massive head of the alien queen in her biomechanical suit.

"Recognize me? You've been in my head too long," Whitmore said.

Down below, David stared at the monitor. The queen's ship was approaching the edge of the trap.

"Come on. Do it, Tom. Do it," he whispered, eager for Whitmore to get in place.

Bam! The queen's ship collided with the energy field. The queen rocked from the collision.

"On behalf of the planet Earth, happy Fourth of July!" Whitmore said.

He pulled the trigger, activating the nuclear bombs.

Kaboom!

Patricia watched from her fighter, tears streaming down her face, as a tremendous blinding light erupted from the queen's ship.

The powerful blast hit the shields, fizzling out on contact. The queen's ship crashed to the desert ground.

President Adams's voice came over David's radio. "Do we have confirmation, Levinson?"

David looked up as the dust clouds began to settle. "I think it's safe to say we got her, Mr. President," he replied. Then he turned to his father and hugged him.

"Who are they?" David asked, pointing to Sam, Felix, Bobby, Daisy, and all the campers.

"Fans!" Julius replied with a smile. "This is Sam, my navigator, and her brothers, Felix and Bobby—"

As Julius spoke, one of the campers was taking a selfie, the downed queen's ship in the background. Then his eyes got wide.

"Excuse me, mister," he said, tugging on David's arm. "Um, is that supposed to happen?"

They all turned—to see the alien queen, two hundred feet tall, towering over the desert.

She had survived.

"She has her own shield," David realized. "Okay, back on the bus, kids! Everyone, on the bus!"

They all quickly obeyed David. But Daisy realized Ginger the dog wasn't around.

"What about Ginger?" Daisy asked.

Sam saw the small dog bravely racing toward the alien

queen, barking. Sam ran to her and scooped her up in her arms. Then she sprinted back to the bus and jumped on board.

David stepped on the gas, and the bus pealed off across the salt flats. The queen chased after them like a dinosaur in pursuit of its prey.

From the radio, President Adams gave him the status. "David, six minutes until Earth's core breach."

Elsewhere, alien fighters shot down the destroyer cannon protecting Area 51. The cannon came crashing into the Area 51 prison wing. The impact knocked the two prison techs off their chairs. When they got to their feet, they saw that the window overlooking the cell blocks was smashed.

One of the techs raced to the monitors. On almost every screen, alien prisoners were escaping from their cells.

"Command, we have a breach!" the tech reported.

President Adams answered him. "How many do you think?"

"At least two dozen, sir," the tech replied.

"Under no circumstances can they see the sphere!" Adams ordered. "Do whatever it takes!"

Sirens blared throughout the alien prison. One of the techs grabbed blasters from the weapons locker while the other tech closed the doors leading to the isolation chamber.

Inside the chamber, the sphere dropped to the ground.

"That can't be good," Dr. Okun said.

Outside, David continued to speed across the desert, but the alien queen was almost on top of him. Patricia followed in her fighter, firing at the queen. But her bio-mechanical shield was immune to the blasts.

"All pilots, target the queen!" she radioed. "Unload everything you've got!"

Bang! Bang! Bang! The remaining pilots converged on the queen. They couldn't take her out, but her shield flickered and she stumbled. The bus gained a little bit of distance.

The queen recovered and quickly closed in. Without warning, she leaped into the air and vaulted over the bus!

Wham! The queen landed in front of the bus. David swerved away at the last second.

The air hummed as the queen's alien fighters zoomed in to protect her from Patricia and the other pilots. The sky erupted in laser blasts as the alien and human pilots targeted one another.

Patricia avoided a blast and kept her sights on the queen.

Boom! Patricia hit the queen with a barrage of fire.

The queen's shield flickered some more—and then completely fizzled out!

"Her shields are down!" Patricia yelled.

She made a sharp curve and fired on the queen again. This time the queen leaped at Patricia's fighter, using her enormous hand to catch the tail wing. Patricia's fighter tumbled toward the ground.

She hit the eject button just in time and spiraled out of the fighter and across the desert.

CHAPTER 25

Patricia looked up from her ejected pilot's seat and saw the queen stampeding toward her. She pulled at her seat straps but couldn't get free. Then, all of a sudden, the queen veered off-balance, shot by the fire of . . . an alien fighter? Patricia, watched, puzzled, as the fighters blasted the queen again and again.

She had no idea Jake and Dylan were in the pilot's seats.

Dylan spoke into the radio. "This is Captain Hiller. We've captured a couple of alien fighters. Don't shoot at us!"

"Roger that," President Adams told him. "You've got four minutes and ten seconds to destroy the queen, or the Earth's core fails."

"Copy that," Jake replied. "No pressure."

Dylan and Jake piloted their fighter straight toward

the queen, Rain and Charlie's fighter close behind.

Inside Area 51, Dikembe and Floyd heard the radio call for help from the prison monitor station. They grabbed blasters and raced to the prison.

When they got there, the door was closed.

"Open the door!" Dikembe yelled. "We're here."

No one answered. They couldn't.

The aliens had already breached the monitor room. One of the aliens had controlled a prison tech, making him unlock the isolation chamber.

Inside the chamber, Dr. Okun and Dr. Isaacs turned to see the doors opening. Slowly, an alien peered around the corner.

It discovered the sphere.

Dr. Okun grabbed his head in pain as the alien soldier sent a telepathic message to the queen. Out in the corridor, Dikembe felt the same pain.

And outside, the queen stopped in her tracks. She turned away from the action and raced toward Area 51.

Meanwhile, the controls in the alien fighters stopped responding to the humans' commands.

"Charlie, do something!" Jake said, panicking.

"I can't," Charlie answered. "She's taken control of our systems! It's the hive mind!"

Jake watched as thousands of other alien fighters

began to swarm around the queen. "Looks like we're not the only ones."

David watched from the school bus. "They are trying to protect her," he realized.

"Then why are we following her?" Julius asked, leaning over the driver's seat.

"Stay behind the yellow line, Dad!" David scolded.

Inside Area 51, two aliens wielding blasters entered the isolation chamber. Dr. Okun reached for Dr. Isaacs's hand. They dove for cover as the aliens opened fire, shattering the last wall of glass protecting the doctors—and the sphere.

Outside the chamber, Dikembe and Floyd heard the blasts. Floyd pushed Dikembe aside and fired at the control panel. The door opened, and Floyd burst into the isolation chamber, firing blindly. When the smoke settled, he saw he'd taken out four aliens.

He was about to cheer when he felt a tentacle wrap around his ankle.

Slice! Dikembe severed the tentacle and then finished off the alien.

Dr. Okun poked his head up from behind a metal table. He smiled when he saw his rescuers. "Baby, we're saved!" he called to Dr. Isaacs.

Then he heard a groan. He looked down to see

Dr. Isaacs, shot in the chest by a blaster. Okun fell to his knees.

"You're gonna be okay. We'll get you to sick bay and fix you up," he said, tears in his eyes.

"I'm not gonna make it," Isaacs said, his voice hoarse.

Okun held his hand. "You can't go. Don't say that. Who's going to water my orchids?"

Isaacs managed a smile. "Who's gonna remind you to put your pants on in the morning?"

Then he took one last labored breath. His eyes closed. Dr. Okun lowered his head, sobbing. "Oh no, baby, no," he said softly.

Outside, the queen had reached the prison building. Her biomechanical suit was battered, but she was undaunted, furiously ripping away at the roof.

Soldiers on the ground hit her with laser blasts. To protect herself, she summoned her fighters to swarm around her and act as a shield.

David pulled the school bus up to Area 51. He, Julius, and the kids watched as the queen ripped into the prison building.

"That's close enough, David," Julius told him.

Dylan, Jake, Rain, and Charlie were helpless in their useless alien fighters.

"We gotta get out of this tornado!" yelled Dylan.

Something about what Dylan said gave Jake an idea. "Every tornado has an eye, right? If we wanna get a shot at her, we gotta get up there."

"You're kidding, right?" asked Charlie. "We have no manual controls left!"

But Jake wouldn't take no for an answer. "Does this thing have a fusion drive?"

Charlie was shocked at what Jake was suggesting. "Are you nuts? The fusion drive is made for outer space. Down here we'll burn up!"

"So that's a yes," Jake continued. "Just a short burst. I think it's our only chance."

Over the radio, a tech informed them that they had only two more minutes until the Earth's core was breached.

"Dylan, you're ranking officer," Jake said. "It's your call."

Dylan smiled. "You nearly killed me once. I survived that. Rain, are you in?"

Rain nodded. "On three," she said.

The pilots reached for the fusion drive switch.

"One . . . two . . . three," Dylan counted.

The alien fighters burst through the pack. Two miles above Earth, the fighters came out of fusion drive.

"Still alive!" Jake cried out.

"And our controls are back!" Dylan noticed.

But it wasn't all good news. The fighters began to plummet back to Earth. Their engines were fried!

Inside the isolation chamber, Dikembe, Floyd, and Okun defended the sphere from another round of escaped alien prisoners. Okun fought like a man possessed, tears running down his face as he fired blast after blast.

When the last alien went down, Dikembe put his arm around the scientist.

"It's over, my friend," he said.

"They're dead! We killed all of them!" Floyd cried.

Then the ceiling peeled back right above them. They all looked up to see a massive alien claw. It reached through the hole in the ceiling and picked up the sphere.

"Except that one," Floyd said.

Towering over Area 51, the queen held the sphere up to her face. Her race had hunted the sphere for thousands of years.

Now the hunt was over.

Zoom! The queen's head jerked to see one of her own fighters flying right toward her!

Dylan was in the pilot's seat. Jake was back in the gunner's seat.

"We only get one shot at this," Dylan told Jake. "Make it count."

Boom! Jake fired, blasting the queen square in the chest. She tumbled backward, still cradling the sphere in her claw.

Charlie fired next and then Jake fired again. The attack tore through the queen's already-weakened bio-mechanical shield.

But the fighters were damaged too. They were losing altitude. There wasn't anything more they could do.

From the bus window, David, Julius, and the kids watched the fighters go down. But the queen was going down too. The sphere rolled out of her claw. Julius and the kids cheered. David grabbed the binoculars to get a better look. He saw the queen desperately wriggling out of her destroyed biomechanical suit. She staggered to her feet, an enormous, slimy creature with translucent skin. Sticky fluid oozed from her chest. She staggered toward the sphere.

"Not again," David said. There were only twenty seconds left before the Earth's core was breached.

David started the engine. He floored it and steered the bus toward the queen.

"David, a school bus full of children is not a weapon!" his father told him. But David had no choice. He had to reach the queen and save Earth.

The queen was still trying to grab the sphere. David

pounded on the gas, and the bus went even faster.

Clang! The bus ran into the sphere, sending it flying across the desert.

Then *splat!* The bus ran into the queen.

Boom! The force of the crash caused her head to explode. Gooey alien blood covered the bus. From inside, Julius and the kids stood up and peered out the windows.

Without their queen, the remaining alien fighters began to break apart. In the Atlantic Ocean, the drill went dark and stopped. The Earth's core was safe. They had destroyed the queen in time!

"Not bad. Not bad at all," President Adams said as everyone celebrated.

CHAPTER 26

Patricia walked toward two smoldering alien fighters on the desert ground. She could hear noises from inside.

She drew her weapon, waiting for the ships to open fire on her, but it never came. The ramp door opened, and a voice came from inside the fighter.

"Whoa! Whoa!"

She lowered her weapon, stunned. Jake poked his head out of the fighter.

"Jake!"

He jumped off the ship and she ran into his arms. Dylan emerged too and smiled at Patricia.

Charlie and Rain climbed out of their fighter and watched the scene.

"Maybe we should try that," he said.

"Dinner first," Rain replied.

Charlie pumped his fist in the air. "Yes!"

Nearby, David, Julius, and the kids got off the bus. An ESD vehicle pulled up, carrying Catherine and President Adams. They stepped out and approached David.

"Director Levinson. Well done," Adams said.

David nodded. "Thank you, Mr. President." He looked over at Catherine. "Catherine, I—"

"Don't say anything." She grinned. "You're just going to ruin it."

David leaned in to kiss her when Julius walked up. "Who are you?" he asked Catherine. "David didn't say anything about a beautiful woman in his life. I'm Julius, his father."

Catherine smiled. "I'm Catherine Marceaux. It's nice to meet you."

"Dad, would you give us a minute?" David asked.

"I was never here," Julius said, holding up his hands.

He walked back over to Sam, Bobby, Felix, and Daisy.

"I've been thinking, maybe you guys should stay with me for a little while," he said.

"I'd like that," Sam replied. "And you owe me a car."

A crowd of survivors came streaming out of Area 51, curious to see the fallen queen for themselves. Dikembe and Floyd ran out, followed by Dr. Okun. He raced to the sphere and placed his hands on it.

"Are you okay?" he asked it.

The sphere began to hover.

I am. Thanks to you. You are a remarkable species.

Floyd turned to Dikembe and held up his alien blaster. "You think they'll let me keep this?"

Dikembe nodded. "You have the heart of a warrior."

"That's the nicest thing anyone's ever said to me," Floyd said.

Dikembe didn't respond. He was looking ahead to where Jake, Patricia, Dylan, Charlie, and Rain were approaching.

"Great job!" President Adams said, saluting them, and the five heroes saluted back.

Then a booming sound rocked the desert, and everyone looked up to the sky to see the alien mother ship leaving Earth.

"Is that all you got?" Dylan called after it, and everyone cheered.

Dr. Okun walked up to David, accompanied by the floating sphere.

"Dr. Levinson! You wouldn't believe what kind of weapons this thing has on its hard drive," he said. "It wants us to lead their galactic resistance."

"What do you mean?" David asked.

"Two words," replied Dr. Okun. "Interstellar travel."

President Adams nodded. "Take the fight to them."

"I was getting bored of this planet anyway," Dylan chimed in.

Jake grinned. "When do we leave?"

"We're gonna kick some serious alien butt!" Dr. Okun cheered.